DAISY:

Not Your Average Super-sleuth!

The Twelfth One

The Pointing Finger

R T GREEN

Other books...

The Daisy Morrow Series:

The first one – The Root of All Evil
The second one – The Strange Case of the Exploding Dolly-trolley
The third one – A Very Unexpected African Adventure
The fourth one - Pirates of Great Yarmouth: Curse of the Crimson Heart
The fifth One – The terrifying Tale of the Homesick Scarecrow
The sixth one – Call of Duty: The Wiltingham Enigma
The seventh one – Christmas in the Manor Born
The eighth one: The Shanghai Shadow
The ninth one – Some Like It Tepid
The tenth one – Waltzing Matilda
The eleventh one – The Wiltingham Incident
The Throwback Prequel: When Daisy Met Aidan
The Box Set – books 1-3
The Second Box Set – books 4-6 plus the Prequel
The Third box set – books 7-9

The Sandie Shaw series:

Book 1 – Murder at the Green Mill
Book 2 – Christmas in Chicago is Murder
Book 3 – An American in Windsor
Book 4 – Springtime in Chicago
Book 5 – Murder on the Miami Express
Book 6 – The Family
The First box set – books 1-3
The Second Box Set – books 4-6

The Starstruck Series -

Starstruck: Somewhere to call Home
Starstruck: The Prequel
(Time to say Goodbye)
Starstruck: The Disappearance of Becca

Starstruck: The Rock
Starstruck: Ghouls, Ghouls and Evil Spirits
Starstruck: The Combo – books 1-3

The Raven Series –

Raven: No Angel!
Raven: Unstoppable
Raven: Black Rose
Raven: The Combo – books 1-3

Somewhere Only She Knows
Timeless
Ballistic
Cry of an Angel
The Hand of Time
Wisp
The Standalones

As Richie Green –

Pale Moon: Season 1:

Episode 1: Rising
Episode 2: Falling
Episode 3: Broken
Episode 4: Phoenix
Episode 5: Jealousy
Episode 6: Homecoming
Episode 7: Fearless
Episode 8: Infinity

Season 2:

Episode 9: Phantom
Episode 10: Endgame
Episode 11: Desperation
Episode 12: Feral
Episode 13: Unbreakable
Episode 14: Phenomenal

Episode 15: Newborn
Episode 16: Evermore

Elsie: Book One, Mean Street

Copyright © 2022 R T Green
All rights reserved.

COME AND JOIN US

We'd love you to become a VIP Reader.

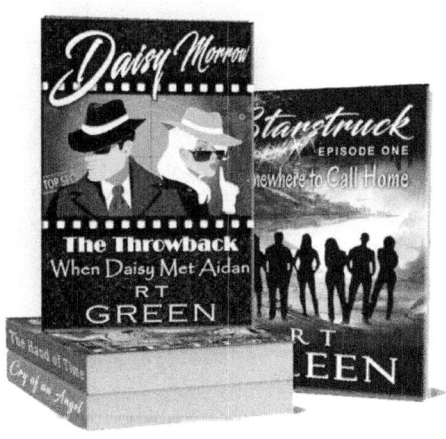

Our intro library is the most generous in publishing!
Join our mail list and grab it all for free.
We really do appreciate every single one of you,
so there's always a freebie or two coming along,
news and updates, advance reads of new releases...

Go here to get started...
rtgreen.net

Contents

COME AND JOIN US 7

Introduction 13

How the Eleventh Adventure Ended... 15

Chapter 44 17

Chapter 45 22

Chapter 46 26

And now the twelfth one – 31

The Pointing Finger 31

Chapter 1 31

Chapter 2 34

Chapter 3 39

Chapter 4 45

Chapter 5 50

Chapter 6 55

Chapter 7 59

Chapter 8 62

Chapter 9 68

Chapter 10 73

Chapter 11   79
Chapter 12   84
Chapter 13   90
Chapter 14   93
Chapter 15   99
Chapter 16   104
Chapter 17   111
Chapter 18   118
Chapter 19   123
Chapter 20   128
Chapter 21   132
Chapter 22   136
Chapter 23   141
Chapter 24   146
Chapter 25   150
Chapter 26   155
Chapter 27   161
Chapter 28   167
Chapter 29   170
Chapter 30   174

Chapter 31 179

Chapter 32 183

Chapter 33 187

Chapter 34 192

Chapter 35 196

Chapter 36 203

Chapter 37 209

Chapter 38 212

Chapter 39 216

Chapter 40 221

Catch the 2022 Christmas Special, 'Here Comes Santa Claus!' 227

'Here Comes Santa Claus' is released in all bookstores, and will also be available direct from our own website, in time for Christmas! 229

Why not give our new series a go? 231

AND DO COME AND JOIN US! 233

The RTG Brand 235

Introduction

The Daisy Morrow series documents the slightly-crazy adventures of our R.E.D. (Retired Extremely Daisy) heroine… she's fun, feisty, kind of wicked, and rather like the other RTG books, she will take you to places you never really expected to go!

This is the twelfth adventure of the hit series. This time Daisy's past catches up with her again, but in an even more worrying way.

Following a recent embarrassing diplomatic mess, MI6 has tasked an obnoxious, thoroughly-unpleasant senior agent with 'cleaning up' their tarnished image.

Part of his task involves scrutinising old missions from before the time the SIS had to be more politically-correct. His eagle-eyes have unearthed a case in 1998 which he believes proves Daisy to be a double agent, and unfortunately for her he has the authority to prosecute.

He's not letting go, but then a couple of discoveries in Daisy's present spook her even more. The darker side of MI6 is out to make an example of her, and ensure they're seen to be doing it.

She realises she has to tread very carefully to prove her innocence, especially as recent events are more fuel for the pointing finger. Daisy can't trust anyone outside her family, other than the one person who might be able to help. The only problem is she's not in the UK.

A trip to the Caribbean is on the cards, but when Daisy and Aidan reach Emerald Island it's not long before they discover something no one in the entire world expected!

Enjoy! Richard, Ann, and the crew

How the Eleventh Adventure Ended...

'We'd better get out of here. It might be gone midnight and in the middle of nowhere, but that lightshow would have been seen for miles. The curious masses will be here anytime now.'

'We'll give the men in black a lift back to their van, which I assume is at the bottom of the hill?' said Daisy.

'Yeah... we wanted to take you by surprise,' said Coop, still unable to speak at his normal volume.

'I think we rather took you by surprise, didn't we?'

'Um... you could say.'

They dropped Coop and Miles at their van. Daisy needed to make sure there were no comebacks. 'So do we need to anticipate getting banged up tomorrow, Coop?' she said pointedly.

Coop threw his hands in the air, so Miles answered for them both. 'You'll be safe, Daisy. As far as we're concerned we were on our way back to London when this happened, so we saw nothing. Did we, Coop?'

'Um... not a thing,' he said meekly.

'That might be a wise move, gentlemen. I don't think your boss would be too pleased to be told you knowingly let an alien life form go.'

'Actually Daisy, I think it was you who knowingly let him go. We weren't even here, remember?'

'Good boys.'

They waved goodbye to the men in black, and then said goodbye to Sarah, who only lived three miles away. Daisy thanked her for her services, above and beyond. 'I really hope you don't get into any trouble for what you did, aiding and abetting an alien, dear.'

She smiled, a little weakly. 'I might find out tomorrow. If I've still got a job I'll let you know.'

'Oh I'm sure we're on your team if it comes to pulling together, Sarah,' said Aidan.

She nodded silently and a little nervously, and drove off.

'Oh dear, I do hope no one finds out what she did,' said Daisy.

Celia and Jack waved hands out of the car windows as they drove past the cottage gate, on their way back to their house. Aidan pulled into the drive, and the three of them headed into the house to greet a relieved and extremely fussy Brutus, who was no doubt wondering where his new friend was.

Daisy explained to him what had happened, still unsure whether he could actually understand her or not. Still trying to believe she was actually explaining what had happened to a cat.

'We should go back to ours, dears,' said Maisie.

Aidan shook his head. 'Maisie, it's gone one in the morning. Sleep here tonight, and then you can go home in the light of day. There's a spare bed now, remember?'

She looked grateful. Aidan made hot chocolate for three, and Maisie disappeared to find sleep. Daisy let out a yawn. 'I guess we should try for sleep too,' she said sadly.

'Our little alien friend got to you, didn't he?' said Aidan as they tramped wearily up the stairs.

'I suppose the place does seem quiet without him.'

'It'll seem even quieter tomorrow when Maisie and Brutus have gone home.'

'Don't remind me. And I still can't believe I took the time to explain things to a cat.'

'I'm sure he appreciated being brought up to speed, Flower.'

'Did you really just say that?'

They walked through the bedroom door. Daisy's hands flew to her face. 'Oh... oh I say...'

Something was there that wasn't there that morning. Two multicoloured knitted bobble-hats sat on the bed, one on each pillow. Daisy wiped away a tear, and picked up her parting gift.

Two words had been knitted into the front. She read them, and burst into tears. Aidan held her close, and read them too. '*Never forget*. I don't think we ever will, do you Flower?'

She found a choky kind of laugh, and put the hat on her head. It was a perfect fit. 'I think there's more than one meaning there, dear.'

Chapter 44

Sarah arrived at Kings Lynn police station a little later the next day. Luckily, given the fact she was extremely late to bed, her shift that morning was an eleven o-clock start.

Burrows wasn't in his office. Her eyes narrowed, even though she knew he often wasn't there. Fear for her job was sparking irrational thoughts that wouldn't stop, and she had to shake them away. Once her boss appeared, he was sharp enough to realise she was worried about something, and she certainly couldn't say a word about what that something was.

Maybe she should pre-empty the event, and resign before she was sacked?

She shook away that thought too, before it festered into reality. No one could possibly be aware what she'd done, after all.

She called over to Williamson. 'No Burrows today?'

He shook his head, looking like he couldn't really care. 'In a meeting with the bosses, I think.'

Sarah's heart skipped a beat. A meeting with the top brass? About her imminent dismissal?

She shook her head, telling herself to stop being so paranoid. It wasn't the first time he'd had meetings of that nature.

She shook her head, sat at her desk, and brought up the internet to see what had made the news about the previous night.

An hour later Burrows shuffled through the squad-room. Sarah tried to convince her head what she was seeing in his craggy face was her freaked-out imagination, but somehow it didn't seem to work. He really didn't look happy.

Then again, he hardly ever did.

As he passed by her desk, he said something that sent her panic levels through the roof. 'Five minutes, Lowry. Then come to my office.'

Five minutes? Three hundred seconds to sit there squirming uncomfortably while her imagination ran riot, despite her telling it not to?

That was just plain cruel. Prolonging her agony, just to be spiteful. She told herself that wasn't the case, that he just needed a little time to shuffle her dismissal papers.

That didn't help much either.

Four minutes later she stood up on heavy legs that really didn't want to take her where they were going to have to. As she struggled to Burrows' door she ran through the words of a request in the mind... how to ask politely if she would be allowed to resign rather than be sacked.

That was the third thing that didn't help much. Officers of the law who broke the rules weren't allowed such concessions.

She tapped the etched glass of the door. The words *'Come in,'* sent shivers through her whole body.

Burrows indicated for her to sit on the chair at the other side of the desk. His eyes were scanning a document in his hands, but she couldn't see what it was. He hadn't said a word since she'd arrived in the office, being supremely cruel again. Sarah began to think that trapped in the lion's enclosure at Africa Alive would be preferable to where she was right then.

After twenty minutes he finally looked up. In reality it was a single minute, but from Sarah's point of view it felt like eternity.

'Constable Lowry.'

'Sir, I...'

'Are you pleased with yourself, Constable?'

'I... no, sir. I can explain...'

'You should be.'

'Um... sorry, sir?'

'You should be pleased with yourself. After you left shift last night, someone you know walked in and asked to see me.'

'Someone I know? Asked to see you?' Sarah mumbled, more confused than she had been for the previous few days.

'Yes. Sister Richards from the covid ward at the Queen Elizabeth.'

Sarah's heart fell through the floor. Her worst fears had come to pass. 'Sir, can I expl...'

'No need, Lowry. Sister Richards told me everything.'

'Oh. I see.'

'You don't look very pleased, Lowry.'

'What is there to be pleased about, sir?'

'Well, going above and beyond and persuading a thief to confess is creditworthy, isn't it?'

'I... *confess?* I don't understand.'

'The sister told me what you did. Making an obviously-fake inventory check while you were at the hospital, and then emphasising the fact that when someone there was caught their life wouldn't be worth living was a quality move, Lowry. You really should have told me what you were planning though.'

'I... I didn't really do anything, sir,' Sarah improvised hastily.

'Please don't do yourself down, Lowry. You obviously gave her the impression you knew what was going on, enough to rattle her conscience and make her confess.'

'I... I did, sir?'

'Yes, you did. And I'm proud of you. Because of you the Kings Lynn police have cracked a medical supplies supply ring on the dark web.'

'Oh... thank you, sir,' said Sarah, her heart beginning to beat again.

'In truth it's not the first time I've been proud of you, Lowry.'

'It... it isn't, sir?' said Sarah disbelievingly.

'No. Despite the fact most of your heroics have involved a certain two interfering pensioners, you have proved yourself more than capable.'

'Um... thank you, sir.'

He passed her the document in his hands. 'So I suggest you fill that in, right now.'

Sarah looked at it through the gloss in her eyes. 'An application for the role of sergeant, sir? I don't understand.'

He actually smiled. 'It's just a formality, Lowry. I've already approved and recommended your application. That's where I was a few minutes ago. I might appear to be an old dinosaur, but credit where it's due.'

'I don't know what to say, sir.'

'I would have done it before, but I felt it wasn't appropriate when your recent injuries were serious enough to put you in a wheelchair for two months. Not that it appeared to curtail your effectiveness.'

'My friends were under siege on Cromer Pier, sir.'

'Indeed. And that tenacious attitude will serve you well. Just be aware that elderly residents who think they're super-sleuths can be more trouble than they're worth. Although I suppose you've already bought the t-shirt on that one.'

'Sir... I can't believe this.'

'Well you need to, and when you've got your brain around my random act of kindness that is totally deserved, get form-filling. I have to go charge a ward sister anyway.'

Chapter 45

In Fern Cottage the next morning, it wasn't an early start. One by one the four of them drifted downstairs, Brutus making sure his human friends didn't sleep too long before giving him his breakfast.

After the rest of them had eaten, Maisie announced she was heading home. Daisy gave her a hug and thanked her for being her, and they said goodbye at the kitchen door.

'I must go straight to say hello to my roses, dears,' she said. 'I haven't said a single word to them for ages. They'll be wondering what's going on.'

'Maisie, they're plants.'

Aidan chuckled. 'Don't knock it, dear. Given what we've discovered in the last few days, they probably are a little worried.'

'Of course they are. I need to give them extra water to make it up to them,' said Maisie, half indignantly.

'I suppose you need to get on the dark web too, and see if any spaceships have come up for sale?'

Maisie looked at Aidan like he was taking the mickey. 'Don't be silly. I don't have that kind of money. Do you realise how much those things go for?'

Aidan shook his head, but decided it might be better to say nothing more. Maisie thanked them both for being there for her and Brutus, and the two of them trotted off.

Daisy wrapped a hand around Aidan's. 'And then there were two.'

Ten minutes later the phone rang. Daisy answered. It was Sarah.

'I just thought I would let you know that in two weeks time I won't be a PC anymore.'

Daisy's heart sank through the floor. 'Oh Sarah... oh no. What can we do?'

She giggled. *'There's no need to do anything. In a fortnight I'll be a sergeant!'*

'Oh... oh, I don't know what to say, other than the fact you thoroughly deserve it. But, um... how?'

'It seems when I illegally stole the covid pills I accidentally put the wind up the ward sister. I didn't know I had, but last night she walked into the station and confessed to being the thief. She told Burrows I'd apparently put the fear of god into her.'

'Oh, that's wonderful... I mean, for you. So Burrows believed you'd done it deliberately?'

'It seems so. I'm still pissed at you for making me do it though.'

'Really, dear? If we hadn't... not that we actually did... you would still have been a constable. Because of Celia and me you've now had a major hike in salary, if I'm not mistaken.'

'Okay, point taken. I still had to go through hell to get there though. Again.'

'You love it, you know you do.'

'Keep believing that, and we'll get though the next adventure.'

'If you say so, dear.'

A half-hour later, the front door knocked. Daisy peered out of the front window, the curtains now drawn fully back. 'Oh no. Dip, it's the men in black.'

He narrowed his eyes, and together they headed into the front hall and opened the door.

'Gentlemen... we were really hoping not to see you again. I thought you'd be back in London by now.'

Coop grinned. 'What, at that time of the night? Nah, we stayed one more night in the hotel. We're heading back in a few minutes.'

'So you just called in here, to grab us and take us back with you to the Tower of London?'

Miles smiled, slightly sympathetically. 'Actually, we just came to say goodbye.'

'In that case, you'd better come in.'

Miles and Coop sat side by side on the sofa. Aidan headed to the kitchen and flicked on the overworked kettle. Daisy decided to play the senility card, just in case.

'Oh gentlemen, you really had me going for a moment there. My old heart is all of a flutter now.'

Coop shook his head. 'Okay Daisy, you can quite with the senile old lady act now. You're not any trouble, and you're not fooling us.'

'Oh... are you sure, Mr. Cooper?'

'If you imitate Miss Marple anymore, I swear I *will* arrest you.'

'Okay, fair enough. I'm not sure I could take being banged up... yes I know, I'm stopping. You just have that effect on me, gentlemen.'

Miles shook his head again, but this time with a slight smile. 'We've decided to forget what we saw last night... haven't we, Coop?'

He threw a hand in the air. 'If you say so, Miles.'

'My partner is still smarting about the fact he saw sense and let Alan go.'

Daisy nodded. 'I know how he feels. But sometimes the greater good, and all that? He'll feel better tomorrow, when his soft side kicks back in and tells him he did the right thing.'

'I don't have a soft side,' Coop complained.

'Sure you do. I saw it last night, and I'm seeing it now.'

'So you're psychic as well?'

Aidan handed the two men coffees. 'No, that's Maisie. And her Klingon cat, of course.'

'Huh?' said Miles.

'If there's an alien cat in the neighbourhood, we need to investigate,' said Coop, clutching at last straws.

'Coop... get real,' said Miles.

'My husband is winding you up, Coop,' said Daisy. 'But even so, you perhaps need to chill a little.'

'I suppose I do,' said Coop reluctantly.

Aidan had a question that had been bugging him for a few days. 'Your codename... DIAL. I assume that stands for something?'

'It does,' said Coop.

Daisy looked thoughtful. 'Department for the Investigation...'

Aidan completed the deduction. 'Might it be... of Alien Life?'

'See, we don't need to tell switched-on pensioners like you,' Coop grinned.

'Makes sense now,' said Daisy quietly.

'Yes, but we do need to tell you we don't officially exist, not outside the SIS anyway.'

'Our lips are sealed, gentlemen. Like yours, it seems.'

Miles agreed. 'Much against my partner's gut feeling, we've agreed that as far as the world knows we, or anyone else, weren't anywhere near Ferret's Hill last night. Much like the hill itself, what happened doesn't really exist. Not officially anyway.'

'There's a lot of speculation in the media. One or two people took distant videos on their phone, although the cloud cover didn't make them very clear.'

'It'll all die down in a few days. There's not a single bit of physical evidence anywhere, unlike Roswell. Then it'll just be a feature on *Stranger Things*,' said Aidan.

'But *we* know, gentlemen.'

'No you don't. You don't know a thing, understand?'

'The issue is though, Coop... we didn't see a thing, as long as you admit to having a soft centre.'

'Who, me?'

'That's the deal.'

Miles sighed. 'Just admit it, Coop. We all know you have, after what didn't happen last night.'

He shrugged his shoulders. 'Okay, okay. You win, Daisy... yet again.'

'Then all's well that ends well, gentlemen.'

Coop finally smiled, shaking his head at the same time. 'And eventually you did get round to calling me Coop.'

Chapter 46

It was a beautiful August night. Daisy and Aidan decided to sip their bedtime hot chocolate on the terrace. Somehow they both needed a little time to gaze at the stars shining brightly above.

'I don't think I'll ever look at the stars the same way ever again, Dip,' said Daisy quietly.

'Nor me. Somehow they have new meaning now.'

'Where do you think our friends are?'

'Oh, somewhere in the Milky Way, heading for infinity and beyond.'

'At least we now know there really is something out there.'

'I guess that makes us privileged Earthlings.'

'That's how it feels right now.'

Aidan took his wife's hand. 'I don't suppose I need to ask what else you're feeling right now, dear?'

'There's no fooling your galactic brain, is there? I miss Alan, already. The cottage feels kind of empty.'

He nodded, and then chuckled. 'Maybe we should get a Klingon cat?'

'Now you are descending into the realms of Star Trek, Dip.'

'Am I?' he said, half-seriously.

The answer took a moment to come. 'A week ago I would have said a remark like that would get me calling the men in white coats, now I'm not so sure.'

'I did discover something new last night though, even if I should have seen it before. Alan and his people are telepathic. Did you notice when he and his family were in that group hug, not a word was actually said? And yet when his wife, or whatever equivalent she was, came up to us, she said thank you like she knew what we'd done.'

Daisy nodded, almost to herself. 'It was a beautiful moment.'

'Yes, I couldn't help but notice the watery eyes.'

She squeezed his hand. 'If they are telepathic, it would explain a few things, like when he said you had to look behind the eyes.'

'That would mean Brutus is telepathic too.'

'Maybe he is. What do we really know, dear?'

'A lot less than we thought we did.'

The conversation died, as they both went back to stargazing, almost like they were searching for a pinprick of moving light that was long gone. Then Daisy broke the silence.

'I think I might take up crocheting again, dear.'

'Oh lord, not another scarf?'

She laughed, and shook her head. 'No, I was thinking of making a stuffed Alan, to give to Brutus as a memento.'

'Somehow I think he'd like that. Something to snuggle up to when he needs a little comfort. Great idea.'

'Maybe I'll make a second one for me.'

'You're soft side is coming to the fore, Flower.'

'Just don't say it's because I'm at that funny age. Having said that, it might be true.'

'True or not, it'll be something to remember him by.'

'I won't ever forget him, Dip.'

'I don't think any of us will. Maisie is rueing the fact she's not rich enough to buy a spaceship and go after him.'

'She'll never be the same either.'

He laughed. 'For sure, we'll never look at her in the same way ever again.'

'Or Brutus.'

The mugs were empty. It was almost midnight. Aidan suggested they stop stargazing and try to find sleep. It wasn't going be easy, given the universal nature of their latest adventure. He gave his wife a gentle kiss, and then smiled.

'Are you going to wear that bobble hat in bed too, Flower?'

She smiled, a little embarrassingly. 'It... it's a little chilly. It's keeping my head warm.'

Aidan stopped himself saying what he'd intended to. Instead he wrapped an arm around his emotional wife as they stood up to head inside, and said something else instead.

'Those words Alan knitted into the front of your hat. *Never forget*. I assume there just wasn't room to add the word *me*?'

Daisy lay her head on his shoulder. 'I suppose so, dear.' Let's go shuggle up.'

They headed inside. Daisy apologised silently to herself for not telling him Alan had never intended the word *me* to be there.

Daisy's personalised bobble hat said exactly what it was intended to.

And now the twelfth one –

The Pointing Finger

Chapter 1

'I miss Alan.'

'We all do, Maisie. He made quite an impression on everyone.'

Maisie clunked her mug back onto the island unit, and gazed thoughtfully to the ceiling. 'Brutus does too. He misses talking with him.'

Aidan shook his head, as he often did when Maisie was around. This time though, it was more aimed at himself. 'Two weeks ago I would have dismissed that as a typical Maisie statement... now I believe every word.'

She glanced to him with a disdainful expression. 'And so you should. Then again, you are just a man.'

'But Daisy thinks...'

Daisy cut him short. 'I believe every word too, Maisie. Especially as we now know he's a Klingon cat.'

Maisie switched the disdainful expression to her friend. 'He's not a Klingon cat, *thank you*. He's every bit as human as you or me.'

Aidan tried to butt in again. 'Cat's aren't hu...'

This time it was Maisie who stopped the words. 'He's not been the same since Alan left.'

'Is that why he's not your usual shadow this morning?'

She nodded. 'He just looked so down in the dumps today. I asked if he wanted to walk round with me, but he said no.'

'I'm saying nothing,' said Aidan, pouring himself a refill.

'I guess having been abducted by aliens, they taught you how to talk to Klingon cats,' said Daisy, not exactly seriously.

'I said, he's not a... oh, forget it. I never did get much sense out of you two.'

'I'm saying nothing,' said Aidan again.

Daisy wasn't letting up. 'I suppose then it's because you're a closet trekkie, Maisie?'

'I have to be in the closet, dear. If it got around the village an eighty-year old was into all things Gene Roddenberry I'd be seen as a little... eccentric.'

'I'm still saying nothing,' said Aidan quietly, into his mug.

'It must have given you a head start while you were in the company of aliens I guess,' grinned Daisy.

Maisie didn't quite share the good-natured ribbing. 'They were so sweet,' she said curtly. 'They just wanted to know where Alan was. Unfortunately, because *you* didn't inform me you were harbouring him, I couldn't tell them.'

'I know. Bad us,' said Daisy ruefully.

'Yes, bad you. I still miss them all though. They reminded me of the Ferengi... just without the obsession for money and the big ears.'

'*Ferengi?*' said Daisy. 'Aren't they just greedy little creatures out for themselves?'

'Oh, so you're a closet trekkie too then?'

Daisy glanced to the floor. 'I might have seen an episode or two of *Deep Space Nine*.'

Aidan finally got an amused word in. 'If Alan did have ears the size of Quark's then Daisy might have had more success ripping off his head,' he chuckled.

'That's not even funny,' said Maisie in a disgruntled kind of way.

Kind of agreeing, Daisy put a hand on her arm. 'As you say, Aidan is just a man. Quark's head might well have come off, but Alan's actually was part of him.'

'Oh... *really*...' Maisie spluttered out, like it was an insult to all things Star Trek.

'Another coffee?' said Aidan in a little voice, trying desperately to change the subject.

'No thank you, Aidan. I think I should go before I get corrupted even further.'

'We weren't being serious, Maisie. We were, Aidan?' said Daisy.

'Um... well...'

Daisy bustled her friend to the kitchen door. 'You should go and give your Kli... Brutus a bit of fuss, Maisie. I'll bring Aidan back down to Earth, promise.'

'Yes, I really think you should. I won't tell Brutus you were talking about ripping Alan's head off.'

'Perhaps not the best idea. Just tell him the mother-ship is back in the Delta quadrant now.'

'You really are a closet trekkie, aren't you dear?'

'Just pretending, Maisie. Oh by the way, would you like a Doctor Who scarf? We've got a few in stock!'

Chapter 2

Daisy and Aidan spent a couple of hours pottering around the house, doing nothing important. Life after Alan had settled back into a normal kind of terrestrial routine, and warm August evenings had reverted to chillier October ones.

The long dry spell had ended too. Rain that hadn't shown itself for over eight weeks suddenly reappeared with a vengeance, together with thunder and lightning to herald its triumphant return. There were a few reports on the TV news of strange objects in the sky over West Norfolk, and one or two phone snaps taken from a distance were pored over for a week or two, but after a while the initial excitement had nowhere to go.

The government slapped a blanket over the whole incident, telling the general public it was all to do with experimental aircraft, and nothing scary or newsworthy had ever happened. Norfolk had always had its fair share of aviation experiments in the past after all, so apart from conspiracy theorists who likened it to Roswell, nobody really cared.

The few residents of Wiltingham who knew the truth decided to keep it zipped, realising if they made waves, life as they knew it would become unbearable. The same couldn't be said about Brutus, who had probably told every cat in the village.

Luckily it was only Maisie and her special skills who could hear what the feline chatter was speculating.

Just after lunch the front door knocked. Daisy glanced to Aidan. 'That can't be Maisie, she just walks straight in through the kitchen door.'

'I guess we'd better see who it is.'

Daisy padded into the front hall and opened the door. In less than a second she'd taken an instant dislike to the man standing there.

'Miss Morrow?' he said curtly.

Daisy frowned. That was a giveaway opening two words, on the basis he clearly wasn't local. 'Or Mrs. Henderson. You choose.'

'Yes, quite. My name is Eric Mildew.'

'Sorry, we're not in the market for damp proofing.'

'Very funny. May I come in, please?'

'Do you work for Rentokil?'

'Certainly not.'

'Then who are you?'

'I'm a senior investigations officer, employed by MI6. Now may I come in?'

Daisy stood aside, her heart missing a beat as she indicated to the man to enter. 'Please do, if you really must.'

He stepped into the hallway, and then gave her a piggy-eyed stare. 'It is not in your best interests to be hostile, Daisy. This is a courtesy call, so please understand it did not have to be made.'

'Um... tea?'

Aidan brewed the man a cup of tea, a frown on his face. Like Daisy, he knew instantly their unexpected visitor wasn't the bearer of good news. The man from MI6 parked himself the sofa, took off his bowler hat, and placed it by his side next to his briefcase. Daisy sat opposite him in one of the armchairs.

A frown creased her brow too. She knew even more than Aidan what she was about to hear wouldn't make easy listening, especially as the guy was dressed in an old-fashioned tweed suit and waistcoat to match. 'So Mr. Mildew, what is this about, because you're obviously not here to sell us bleach?'

She tried to keep the amusement from her tone, which really wasn't amusement at all. Mr. Mildew noticed of course, and didn't seem the slightest bit impressed.

'I suggest you keep the frivolity from your tone, Daisy. I am not here to be mocked.'

'Of course not, Mr. M... Eric. What can I do for you?'

He didn't mince his words, which were delivered with a stony-faced expression. 'You will of course be aware that since the war in Ukraine, and Russia's clear return to the Cold War era, other soviet-sympathetic countries have rekindled their dislike of all things western. As you can imagine, MI6 has suddenly found itself a lot busier than it has been for some time.'

'Don't tell me you're here to re-enlist me?'

He sniggered in a menacing kind of way. 'Don't be ridiculous. You're far too old.'

'Excuse me?'

'Daisy, I'm here for something... well, something quite the opposite, frankly.'

'Now I'm confused.'

'One of the countries we need to pay closer attention to is China, together with the countries it sees as allies. Sadly, in order to be taken seriously as a credible organisation in the current situation, I have been tasked with re-evaluating events from some years ago, to make sure nothing comes back to bite us in the present.'

'So you're reopening old, closed cases, so you can cleanse MI6 of stuff that may have happened way back when?'

He shook his head like a disappointed schoolmaster. 'I had rather assumed you would take that attitude, given your record.'

'Um... my record?'

'You did ruffle a few feathers from time to time, shall we say?'

'Back in the distant past when I was in the field I was one of very few female operatives, Eric. It was obligatory to ruffle a few feathers in order to make an impression.'

'Unfortunately for you, it has come to light that something which happened in the distant past, as you put it, has more serious consequences in the here-and-now.'

Daisy smiled, but there was no humour in it. 'Ah, I see. You believe you've unearthed something I did that happened before MI6 were forced to be more politically-correct, I assume.'

Eric narrowed his eyes. 'I'm afraid that what I have discovered is far more serious than that, Daisy.'

The smile, humourless as it was, faded. When Daisy spoke, the words were formed slowly and deliberately. 'Perhaps you'd better spell out why you are here, Eric.'

'I'm here as a courtesy call, Daisy. Despite the fact you no doubt see me as a meddlesome damp-proofing salesman, I suggest you leave aside your animosity and treat this as a very serious matter.'

She nodded slowly. 'It's my defence mechanism, something that kicks in when I sense danger.'

'Your sixth sense is well-founded in this case. I should make you aware that my team are currently preparing a case against you that will in due course be sent to the Crown Prosecution Service.'

'I would say you can't be serious, but you clearly aren't capable of making jokes.'

Eric shook his head again. 'Still you attempt to be derogatory, Daisy. Perhaps your attitude to me will change if I tell you the case building against you is based on information we have gathered that, in your time working as an MI6 field operative, it appears you acted as a double agent.'

Chapter 3

'What? Now I am going to say you can't be serious.'
'I'm sorry Daisy, the evidence says otherwise.'
'Evidence? What evidence?'
'I'm not obliged to tell you. Official documents will be delivered to you shortly to detail the charges.'
'Oh come on, Eric. You deliver a hammer blow like that and then bugger off to sell Dettol to the next door neighbours?'
'Still you insist on being flippant.'
'Are you surprised? It's totally ridiculous.'
Aidan handed their visitor a cup of tea. 'I can assure you my wife is not, and never has been a double agent, Mr. Mildew.'
'So you know every detail of your wife's employment with MI6, Mr. Henderson?'
'Most of them, yes.'
'Except for the ones she doesn't want you to know.'
'Oh, be serious.'
Daisy grabbed hold of the tea Aidan handed her, and took a large gulp. Her hand was shaking. The next question came out in an equally-shaky kind of way. 'Please tell me how you have come to this conclusion, Eric.'
He sighed, like he really didn't want to. 'I'm not supposed to say anything at this stage, Daisy.'
'But you will, won't you? People like you get off on gloating.'
'May I remind you that attitude isn't helping, Daisy.'
'Sorry. Bit shaken up here.'

'With good reason. Believe me, this matter gives me no pleasure. But MI6 has to clean up its past, and be seen to be doing it.'

'So I'm the fall guy?'

'If you are the fall guy, Daisy, it's because you have somewhere to fall from.'

'According to you.'

'Indeed. And according to the evidence, which I *will* tell you initially relates to what went down in Afghanistan in ninety-eight.'

'Ah.'

Eric narrowed his piggy eyes. 'So it appears that's made you sit up and take notice, Daisy?'

'Of course it has. I made a mistake. It wasn't entirely my fault, we were all duped.'

'Perhaps. But the evidence suggests *you* weren't duped, Daisy. It would appear you were the one who informed Osama bin Laden the US were about to strike the Khost camp with a cruise missile, in order that he had time to substitute a decoy.'

'Me? But... but... I was as shocked as everyone else when I saw it wasn't him in the compound.'

'Were you? Or were you relieved your plan had worked?'

'I'm starting to like you even less, Eric.'

'By the time this is over you may hate me with a vengeance, Daisy. Please remember, I'm only doing my job.'

'Ah yes... the job with the remit to spot every single mistake an operative has ever made, and then blow it up into something it's not.'

'Let us just accept that you and I see my job from different angles, Daisy.'

'Yes. The words witch and hunt come to mind from my angle... respectfully of course.'

'You're still not helping your case.'

'Don't worry, I'll leave that to my legal counsel.'

'Which is the reason for my courtesy call, to give you time to prepare your defence.'

'Forgive me if I can't see much courtesy floating around right now.'

'So you would rather have answered the door one day to a member of the Crown Prosecution team, serving you official papers?'

'Okay, I appreciate how overwhelmingly courteous you are. I still can't see what evidence you have to corroborate me being a traitor to my country.'

'I will admit, you covered your tracks well. However, the evidence does not just relate to the distant past. It also has some connection to events earlier this year.'

'What? I've been retired for twelve years.'

'Hmm... I think Alexandra Robertson would disagree with that, don't you?'

'Ah.'

'Yes, I thought that might press the panic button.'

'You really are an obnoxious little man, aren't you? There's no panic button, just a disgust key.'

'Everything you say will be noted, Daisy, and possibly used against you.'

'Make sure you extract it from your ass first, or no one will hear it. I can explain the Alex connection.'

'No, Daisy. I will explain. In January this year you paid a visit to an ex-colleague, Alexandra Robertson, who it appears was also a double agent, and who then lost her life while you, and no one else, was present at her cottage in the Lake District.'

'How... how do you know that? Only a very few people were privy to that information.'

'My team and I are very thorough. It remains to be seen if you did in fact murder her, but what is certain is that you burned the cottage, and some very expensive tech, to the ground, with the obvious intention of removing all evidence of what you'd done.'

'But... but I wasn't alone. And I did what I did on the orders of MI6.'

'Daisy, you just told me you have been retired for twelve years?'

'Yes, but...'

'You should be informed that MI6 have no knowledge of such an occurrence, or of orders ever being given to a civilian. However, we do believe you are telling the truth about someone else being at the cottage. As we understand it a certain Chinese assassin was present for some of the time, who had intentions to eliminate both you and Alex for treason against China. Shall I go on?'

'Please don't.'

'Dear..?' said Aidan.

'There is one final matter. We have no idea what occurred that particular night, except that for some reason Su Shi Wang did not assassinate you. Indeed, the evidence would suggest you aided her escape from the country, and in so doing made it possible for a criminal wanted in several countries to disappear off the face of the Earth.'

'You should write fiction, Eric.'

'Dear..?' said Aidan.

'I can assure you I deal only in facts, Daisy. Some of which took some unearthing, it has to be said. Something else we know was that an off-duty police officer was seriously injured at that time, which according to official records was an *accident*. I'm sure you can see there are unexplained circumstances, can you not, Daisy?'

'I'm sure there's an explanation.'

'Hmm... sadly I think any explanation might not be so good for you. There is a little more we need to be sure of, but the case against you is quite compelling.'

'So it seems.'

Aidan decided he had to say something. 'Mr. Mildew, I think I should tell you...'

'My husband is just as disgusted as I am, Eric. What he's trying to say is that he's never seen any evidence of a single one of your allegations. Weren't you, *dear*?'

'Well...'

The delightful Eric stood up to leave. 'I shall bid you good day. You clearly have no intention of doing the decent thing and admitting your guilt, so we shall be forced to let the courts decide in due course.' He slipped his bowler hat firmly back onto his head. 'Oh, there's one more thing. In the circumstances, we anticipate that you fleeing the country is a distinct possibility. I am authorised to take this step, so I must ask for your passports, please. Both yours and your husband's.'

'Oh, I say. This is a liberty,' protested Aidan.

'We have to give them to him, dear,' said Daisy in a small voice.

She fetched both their passports from the office drawer and handed them to Eric, who slipped them into his briefcase, thanked them for their cooperation, and headed to the door.

'So how long before I'm thrown in the dungeons at the Tower of London, Eric?' said Daisy.

He turned to look at her like she was being serious. 'Things have come on a bit since those days. You won't need to compete with the rats for your gruel. My case should be concluded in a week or so, after which it's down to the CPS to prosecute in their own good time.' He handed her a small card. 'That is my number. If you see sense and decide to confess all, you can reach me that way. Save us all a lot of upset and time.'

'I'll give it due consideration,' said Daisy quietly.

'Whichever way round, you will be kept informed at every stage. Goodbye.'

He marched determinedly along the path, and he and his bowler disappeared behind the bushes. Aidan turned to his wife, and narrowed his eyes.

'Dear..?' he said again.

Chapter 4

Daisy slumped back into the armchair, like her legs didn't want to support her. 'Things aren't looking too good, Dip,' she said quietly.

'It's all supposition, Flower. You've done nothing wrong.'

'Haven't I? You heard what that jobsworth said... all of what happened in January was true, if you look at it from his angle.'

'I was going to tell Mildew that Rupert was involved, and he also contacted Morrison. That would have helped clear your name.'

'And it would also have revealed that Rupert knew I acted illegally. We both facilitated Su Shi's departure from the UK... after I made sure MI6 didn't catch up with her. If I told the truth now that would lead to MI6 discovering where she was, and I promised her I would never do that.'

'But only Rupert knew what we'd done, and he was the one who arranged her transport after all. *Oh no, surely not...*'

Daisy shook her head. 'No, dear. Rupert wouldn't have grassed... not about our involvement anyway. I'm sure he's already been quizzed, so he would have been forced to give them a few worthwhile facts, but he wouldn't have admitted to being involved in Su Shi's disappearance. That would have incriminated him as well as us.'

'Then who? Mildew must have got his information from somewhere.'

'Yes, he did. Another MI6 jobsworth... Clive Morrison.'

'Who?'

'Rupert's successor. Before you arrived in the Lake District I called Rupert on the satellite phone, to bring him up to speed with what had happened with Alex. Although he'd retired he was the only one who still knew about the Ullswater facility. He said he had to call someone currently in MI6 who was high up enough to make decisions. That someone was Clive Morrison. He called me later, and told me to burn the cottage to the ground.'

'But Mildew said no such conversation had ever taken place.'

'The surveillance facility Alex was managing was so top secret, and at the end became such an embarrassment, Morrison in his infinite wisdom decided he couldn't even admit to his own people he had been informed of its existence.'

'So he's left you to take the rap on your own.'

'No question. Rupert keeping everything so secret hasn't helped either, but in fairness to him, he couldn't have anticipated what would transpire earlier this year. He clearly didn't reveal anything about his involvement in getting Su Shi to Emerald Island, so respect to him for that.'

Aidan shook his head sadly. 'So you and me are the scapegoats, and if you look at the cold hard facts, we *did* actually act illegally.'

'No dear. *I'm* the scapegoat. You're not involved in this.'

He knelt down in front of her, and took her hand. 'Maybe not officially, Flower. But in truth I'm just as guilty, if you can call it that, in making sure the woman who was once nicknamed the Shanghai Shadow disappeared off the face of the Earth. Regardless of what happens now we're in this together, and as far as I'm concerned we're both equally up to our necks in this dirty quicksand.'

Daisy wiped away a tear, and kissed him lovingly. 'I don't know what I'd do without you, you crazy ex-accountant.

Just how much more quicksand am I going to drag you into?'

'It doesn't matter. We've always found our way out before. We'll do it again.'

Daisy was silent for a moment. Then she squeezed Aidan's hand. 'Go on then... ask me the question about Afghanistan you need to ask.'

He chuckled mirthlessly. 'I don't have a single question about nineteen-ninety-eight, dear.'

'Really?'

'Of course I don't. Mildew might think he knows otherwise, but I know for sure.'

'How?'

'Because I know you. You might be infuriatingly-stubborn and in possession of an acid tongue, but there's not a single part of you who could ever be a double agent.'

She lowered her head. 'I love you, you old bugger.'

Aidan prepared them both a little lunch, although neither felt much like eating. Eric Mildew's courteous visit had rather ripped away anything approaching an appetite.

Daisy didn't have a lot to say during the nibbled meal, so as they finally gave up attempting to eat, Aidan said something to break the silence.

'You seem worried, dear. You want to say anything?'

She stood up and headed to the house phone. 'Sorry Dip, I've been mulling things over. I know how these people work, but I just need to confirm something. Please don't make a sound.'

'Dear?'

Daisy picked up the receiver, and dialled an innocent number. 'Oh hello, Sadie. I just wondered if you were open all day today?'

The assistant at the village store sounded a little puzzled. *'Is that you, Daisy? Yes, of course... we're open until six, as always.'*

'Just wanted to make sure, dear. I need a couple of things, but my arthritis is playing up today so I didn't want a wasted trip. See you later.'

She let Sadie put the phone down, but kept the receiver to her ear for a moment longer than she normally would. Then she nodded, and gave Aidan a weak smile. 'You can make all the noise you want now, Dip. I've discovered what I needed to know.'

'What, that the local shop is open, which you knew anyway?' he asked, realising that wasn't the only reason.

'No, that someone is eavesdropping on our house phone. It was just the faintest of extra clicks, but when you know what to listen for, it's kind of telling.'

'Oh my god... how long do you think they've been listening in?'

'Quite a while I would assume. Have we made any giveaway calls do you think?'

'Not for a few weeks, apart from Celia and Sarah.'

'Hmm... I need to warn them. Any mention of close encounters or Su Shi would only give the SIS more fuel.'

'We can call them on our mobiles.'

Daisy shook her head. 'You think they're not monitoring those too?'

'I do now you've said it. Silly me.'

'Give me all the change you've got, dear. I'm going to do what I said and visit the shop. There's a phone box next to the parking area in front of it, if it's still working.'

He threw his hands to the ceiling. 'It's like being back in the Cold War, Flower.'

Daisy found a smile. 'Luckily, back then is when I gained most of my experience in the field. Maybe it will stand me in good stead now.'

'Should I check the house for bugs while you're gone?'

Daisy tapped him on the shoulder. 'You can, but I don't think there'll be any. The only MI6 people who have been in this house this year were Coop and Miles, and they're DIAL, so I can't see they would be involved in this.'

'Even so, it's a bit worrying.'

Daisy grabbed her coat. 'Are you saying that because you're looking at my face, Dip?'

'Maybe.'

Chapter 5

Daisy rolled the electric scooter out of the garage, and set off to the village shop on the opposite side of the large green. She kept an eye out for anyone who might have been watching, but didn't expect to see anyone.

The unrest in Russia and China was keeping MI6 busy, and she already knew their resources would be stretched. Cleaning up their image was important to them, but didn't command the kind of importance the rest of the world needed.

Eric Mildew would likely have been given a small dedicated team, but most of them would for sure spend their days behind a desk in London, not wiling away the hours watching an ex-agent who had likely been tagged as Retired Extremely Dangerous.

Even so, she steered the scooter behind the trees nestling against the side of the beautiful village pond, which was filling up a little since the recent much-needed rains, and then meandered on a random path to reach the post office.

Much of the short journey was across open space, so it was easy to spot anyone who might have been following. As she suspected, no one was. She shook her head, trying to dislodge the paranoia that seemed to be dictating her actions. If she was going to clear her name it had no place being there, but at the same time, warning those who might also have had their phones bugged was a necessary part of understanding where the land lay.

She said hello to Sadie as she bought a couple of items, and then snuck into the phone box. It was working. She checked Sarah's number on her mobile, and then called it from the public phone. She answered, sounding a little puzzled.

'Hello?'

'Sarah, it's Daisy.'

'Daisy? Where are you? I don't recognise the number.'

'It doesn't matter. Something's going down, Sarah. It might be best if you don't call Aidan or me on the landline or the mobiles for now.'

'Daisy? You're scaring me again.'

'It wouldn't be the first time.'

'You can say that again. I guess you don't want to talk over the phone?'

'Not really. If you want to pop in sometime we'll bring you up to speed.'

'We'll come this evening. It sounds like it can't wait.'

'We? I take it you mean you and Rob?'

'Um, yes. We were going out for a meal. But this sounds more urgent.'

'Can't disagree. Come and have your meal at ours. We just can't guarantee you two romantic privacy, of course.'

'That's the last thing I need when you're obviously in some kind of trouble. Seven?'

Daisy climbed back aboard the scooter, and headed to her next destination. Celia and Jack's house, a little further along Walcotts Lane, was also the office of the newly-formed Henderson Detective Agency. When Daisy and Aidan decided to take more of a back seat, something which right then was looking more and more unlikely, they'd set up the agency with their daughter and her partner, intending the younger ones to do more of the physical side of investigating.

Mildew and his small team would for sure know of its existence, and exactly who had a role in it. He likely didn't know Celia and Jack were involved in the events in the Lake District, but a careless remark over the phone would soon implicate them.

Daisy had to make sure that didn't happen.

Both of them were horrified when Daisy brought them up to speed. Celia suggested they make it an evening meal for six, and Daisy agreed. Somehow, even though she knew it wouldn't make the slightest difference in the grand scheme of things, somehow she needed the comfort of safety in numbers.

'Surely they can't think you were ever disloyal, mum?'

'I broke the rules a few times, dear, back when it was more permitted to break them.'

'Yes, but...'

'And I ignored Clive Morrison's instructions to keep Su Shi at the cottage site so MI6 could arrest her and look good.'

'But you were the one who did all the work.'

'And I then arranged for her to be transported to a tiny island in the Caribbean, so a wanted criminal could escape.'

'But... Rupert was involved too...'

'Unofficially, yes.'

'I can't believe he'd do this to you.'

'Celia... he was obviously interrogated by the magnificent Mildew. Rupert would have deduced what he already knew from the questions he was asked, so he worked out he had to give him something. He gave out the bare minimum he could get away with, but still kept a lot back. It's the ladder-climbing Morrison I blame.'

'Yes, the worm who knew nothing.'

'Sadly, dear, these days MI6 is full of them. The 007s are a very minor part of the chain in the present-day SIS.'

'It stinks.'

'Yes it does. I am so glad I'm out of it. Well, kind of out of it.'

Jack shook his head. 'It's not looking so good for you, Daisy.'

'Jack?'

'Face facts, darling. I don't mean to heap any more crap onto this, but the whole chain of events in January does point to only one thing.'

Aidan fixed a cold stare into Jack. 'So you believe my wife was a double agent then?'

'No. No, of course not. Oh hell, I'm digging myself a deeper hole here, aren't I? I meant, if you look at it from Mildew's angle, what happened in January could appear to back up his insane claim Daisy was a double agent.'

Daisy nodded. 'I appreciate your devotion, guys, but Jack has hit the nail on the head. What I did earlier this year was morally right, but legally wrong. Now it's come back to bite me.'

'It still doesn't mean you were a double agent in ninety-eight, mum. Or ever, come to that.'

'Doesn't it? You ever heard of perception?'

'You'd better explain, mum.'

'You only have to look at social media. Someone posts their opinion about a celebrity, together with a picture that out of context says nothing, but when the person who posts it points out something that could be taken two ways, then the trolls freak out. Suddenly one person's twisted opinion becomes fact. Then someone else posts another perfectly-innocent picture, which is tagged as 'proof' the trolls are right, and that celebrity is ruined, all through one person's vindictiveness.'

'So that poster is Mildew, and what happened in the Lake District is his vindication you were a double agent?'

'Of course. Look at Kim Philby. It was speculation in the New York Times, the social media of its day, which led to suspicions of his communist connections. If it wasn't for a public outcry he might have got away with it.'

'But he actually *was* a double agent, Flower.'

'Indeed he was, but did it really matter? Once those in authority started to believe he might have been, every aspect of his life was examined and re-examined, over and over. It could have gone either way, whether he actually was or wasn't guilty.'

'So mum, is there anything in your life that in the wrong hands could point to you being guilty?'

'If you apply the social-media principle, yes. I never was guilty of disloyalty of course, but back in those days we got away with things that are looked upon differently now.'

'So if someone examines them with present-day eyes, they could well assume you were not exactly innocent?'

'Me and every other field agent, yes.'

'But you've been chosen as an example.'

'Sadly, Mildew seems to uphold the dinosaur principle that women had no place in MI6. He does wear a bowler hat after all.'

'*Seriously?*' said Celia. 'Nobody wears bowler hats anymore.'

'Except Mildew.'

Aidan shook his head. 'Perhaps Jack is right.'

'I think he's spot on, yes.'

Chapter 6

'I'm not sure there's much we can do as police,' said Rob. 'The SIS are a law unto themselves. Always were, and likely always will be.'

'I'm so sorry, Daisy,' said Sarah.

'It's okay. I always knew they were above the law. That's why we always got away with so much.'

Sarah glanced to Rob. 'We have to do something. Can't we look into Morrison and Mildew's affairs, find some dirt?'

Rob shook his head. 'SIS records are as secure as the crown jewels, Sarah. The likes of us would never get anywhere near, and even if we tried that might just make matters worse, because they'd know it was us.'

Daisy put a hand on his arm. 'Rob, I wouldn't let you get involved anyway. Your career is just taking off, and something like this could see you back on the beat, or worse. It's only because you met Sarah at Cromer Pier you're even here now.'

He squeezed Sarah's hand as he smiled to her. 'And I'm so glad I got the chance to push your wheelchair around.'

She giggled. 'I'm so glad I gave you the chance to do more than that, Rob.'

Aidan cleared his throat unconvincingly. 'Yes well, my wife is right. It's hard to see anyone can do anything right now.'

'But we have to do something, dad.'

Daisy threw her eyes to the ceiling. 'All we can do right now is stay vigilant. I don't want any of you calling us here with the phone being bugged, and it's a virtual certainty our mobiles are too. So any communication is strictly face to face, okay? No emails or Whatsapp on the PC either.'

'Hell, it's like being in prison.'

'Yes, and we've been incarcerated without knowing it for an unspecified period of time, it would seem.'

'Maybe it's a good thing none of what happened in the Lake District has been spoken about over the phone for months,' said Jack.

'That's a yes. Now I just need to work out what I do next.'

'Other than call our solicitor,' said Aidan quietly.

'We're not there yet. But I need to know exactly what's been said... or more to the point, *not* said. Morbid Mildew could well have not told us everything.'

'You're referring to Rupert, I assume?' said Aidan, knowing his wife too well.

'Yes. I need to know what he didn't say.'

'Yes, *we* do,' Aidan agreed. 'But we can't call him, it's too risky. No doubt they're bugging his phone too.'

'Of course they are. He's well aware he's done things for which he can be held accountable too, so he'll be on alert. I'm surprised he's not appeared on our doorstep before now.'

'He might only have been interrogated in the last couple of days, and he could also suspect he's being watched. He might be feeling like a prisoner too right now.'

'You're not wrong, Dip. In the morning we need to go visit him in Wroxham, but for our sake and his we can't be seen doing it.'

'Fatigues and jungle camouflage then, dear?'

'Oh Dip, you know me so well.'

Daisy didn't have much to say as she and Aidan sat side by side in bed, drinking hot chocolate that somehow seemed more comforting than ever.

'Penny for them, dear?'

'I was just thinking.'

'Yes, I can see the steam from your ears mingling with the steam from your mug.'

She chuckled. 'We'll go and see Rupert in the morning, but he can't really help us without implicating himself, and that would just prove Mildew right anyway.'

'At least we'll know what the bowler-hatted Rottweiler knows... or doesn't know, more to the point.'

'I can't see he knows about Su Shi's secret flight to Trinidad, otherwise both Rupert and me would have been arrested by now.'

'Agreed. But in truth dear, there's a few more incidents over the last eighteen months Rupert could have let slip about.'

Daisy shook her head. 'No. Apart from the fact he agrees with me the SIS has become a lot more self-centred, Rupert would be aware anything he says of that nature would implicate him along with us. I need to know what he *didn't* say, not what he actually said.'

'So we'll no doubt get that information tomorrow, but it won't help us clear your name.'

'No it won't. I was actually deep in thought about something else.'

'Something else?'

'Well, *someone* else perhaps.'

On what he thought was his wife's wavelength again, Aidan asked a leading question. 'My brother? I know he built the tech they installed in the Lake District, but he told me he had no idea where they'd deployed it once it was built. I can't see how he could help.'

'No, Charlie is unlikely to be much use. And we can't call him, just in case they're bugging him too. We might have to go to Emerald Island in person, dear.'

'Flower, you just said he likely can't help. And in case you've forgotten, our passports have been confiscated... even if they hadn't, Mildew would soon know where we'd gone anyway.'

'Which is the second reason we need to speak to Rupert.'

'Dear, you surely can't be suggesting..?'

'My gut tells me we need a secret trip to the Caribbean. This is last chance saloon, Dip, but it's all I can come up with. Rupert is the only one we know with the contacts to arrange the flight we need. Charlie can't help us, but someone else who's on Emerald Island just might be able to.'

'You don't mean..?'

'It's a long shot, dear, but the only vague hope we have of me avoiding spending the rest of my life in prison is Su Shi.'

Chapter 7

'I was joking about the jungle camouflage, Flower.'

Daisy glanced round at Aidan's slightly-breathless words. 'Dear, you know if Morbid Mildew has stationed someone outside Rupert's house he'll know we've been to see him. You think he won't add that to his list of reasons why me and everyone associated with me were double agents?'

'Yes, I know that. But I'm still not sure bits of privet hedge fastened to our woolly hats are really necessary. We're not likely to come across murderous guerrillas in the Wroxham woods.'

'Just run with it, Dip. I'm in my element here.' Daisy let out a cheeky grin as she eyed Aidan up and down. 'And actually, you look quite fetching dressed in dark green jeans and jumper.'

'Stop trying to butter me up. You're actually enjoying this, aren't you?'

'Noo... well, maybe a little. It brings back memories.'

'Shall we just get on with it, and do what we came to do?'

Daisy had insisted they drove right past Rupert's house in The Avenues, looking for suspect vehicles. They parked in the boatyard car park a quarter of a mile away. Between the yacht manufacturers and Rupert's house was a small wood, and the rear gardens of the houses on the left side of the elegant road backed onto it.

As far as she was concerned it was their hidden way in, when they didn't want anyone to know they were there. Aidan was most probably right, they didn't really need their heads adorned with half a privet bush, or to sneak through the not-very-dense woodland like they were behind enemy lines... but old habits die hard.

It was a brief moment of vaguely light relief to a dark scenario which didn't have much else to recommend it... and Daisy was kind of enjoying it.

At least she was, until they reached Rupert's six-foot fence, and the gate in it that was bolted from the inside.

'Cup your hands, Dip.'

'Seriously?'

'Well we can hardly screech *"cooee"* like Maisie, can we?' she hissed.

'Why not? That always gets our attention.'

'Yes, and right now it will also attract the attention of anyone snooping around.'

'I think you're getting a little paranoid, dear.'

'Do you blame me? I'm the one about to be tried for treason, remember?'

'I suppose you have a point.'

'Yes, a very good one. So cup your hands and close your mouth.'

Aidan shook his head for the umpteenth time that morning, but cupped his hands anyway. Daisy dropped a foot into his cradle, and reached for the top of the fence.

'Wow... he's got a big pond.'

Daisy wasn't exactly heavy, but Aidan had been an accountant all his life after all. 'Will you get on with it? I can't hold you up forever.'

'Wimp. Okay, I'm going over.'

'Please be careful.'

'Dip, I've done this a hundred times before.'

He was about to say she might have done, except they were all a long time ago, but then Daisy disappeared from sight behind the other side of the fence. That was followed a millisecond later by a sickening thud, which was then followed by a painful-sounding *'Oww. Bugger.'*

'Are you alright, dear?' Aidan called.

'No... that friggin' fence was really high.'

'Dear, it's a standard six-foot...'

'Stop splitting hairs. I'm hobbling to the gate now and drawing back the bolt, despite my excruciating pain.'

He heard the bolt grate aside, and seconds later Daisy's slightly-embarrassed face appeared as she swung the gate open. 'I guess I'm not as agile as I used to be, dear,' she said ruefully, forcing a smile and removing a strand of privet from in front of her face.

'At least you haven't broken anything... have you?'

'Not sure. We'll head to the Norfolk and Norwich when we're done here and get an x-ray.'

'You... you are joking?'

'Course I am. Apart from a fracture to my pride, and they haven't invented a scan for that yet.'

He gave her a quick hug. 'It's the thought that counts, Flower. You were after all the one brave enough to fall heavily to the ground on the other side of the fence so you could open the gate and avoid me doing the same.'

'Is that a dubious compliment, dear?'

'You decide.'

'Then I shall take it as both a compliment and an observation about my advancing years, dear.'

'Your call.'

Aidan was about to say something else a lot soppier, but he didn't get the chance. A sharp cry filled their ears, and as he looked up and Daisy glanced around hurriedly, they saw someone standing thirty feet away with a raised cricket bat in his hands. *'Stay where you are!'*

Chapter 8

'*Daisy? Aidan?* What the hell?'
'Hello Rupert. We thought we'd pop in for a coffee.'
'This isn't a commando raid then?'
'Very funny. Please lower that cricket bat now.'
He lowered the bat. 'I might have guessed you'd pull a crazy stunt like this.'
'Oh, you know me too well, Rupert. But if you'd guessed I would then you must have good reason.'
'I suppose the bowler-hatted worm came to see you as well then?'
'The fact we're here gives you the answer to that. We *really* could do with a coffee though, so are you going to ask us in?'
'If you take that ridiculous hedge out of your hats first.'
'Consider it done.'
Daisy and Aidan followed Rupert into the kitchen, doing what he'd asked and removing the foliage. He flicked on the kettle as they sat down at the kitchen table, one of them a little more gingerly than the other.
'My wife is in Norwich, doing a little shopping. Rather luckily, given the state of you two.'
'We can't be too careful, Rupert. Morbid Mildew might have stationed someone outside.'
'I doubt it. MI6 must be a little stretched right now, so I can't imagine they gave him much of a team.'
'From what we saw, he doesn't really need one. Assumptions are plenty enough for him.'
He nodded slowly. 'You didn't need to go to all that... trouble, Daisy. I was coming to see you this afternoon.'

'Which by default means you also see this as serious then?'

'It is serious. Not that there's any truth in his historic allegations, but unfortunately for you and me the more recent rule-bending we were both part of carries just as much risk of incarceration.'

'You mean like transporting Charlie and Danielle to an undisclosed location, together with his AI creation that could have changed the world, and then doing the same for a wanted international criminal.'

'When you put it like that, Daisy, you have a lot to answer for.'

'Me? You arranged it all... unofficially of course, Rupert.'

'At your request. And against my better judgment, it has to be said.'

'You still did it though.'

'You can be very persuasive.'

'Tell me about it,' said Aidan, pulling a stray piece of privet from his woolly hat.

Daisy shook her head, knowing they were both right. 'Okay, so we've established it's all my fault. Right now though, if Mildew unearths my... *our* secret activities, we're both in trouble. We came to find out what you said to him.'

Rupert handed them coffees, and sat down at the opposite side of the table. 'I said only what I had to. I told him about the secret installation in the Lake District, and some of what had gone down there. I also had to inform him about Su Shi and the Chinese assassination squad, otherwise once he discovered the facts he would have arrested you for murdering Alex.'

'I realise that. So how much did you tell him about Su Shi?'

'Not enough to implicate you or me. I said after the incident involving Sarah you and Su Shi parted company, and you never saw her again. That should have been enough to shut him up and clear us both.'

'Except Clive Morrison denied all knowledge he knew anything about the Lake District installation, including the fact it ever existed.'

Rupert lowered his head. 'I didn't know that, but I might have guessed. The fact it had been so easily compromised by the Chinese, and was the source of acute embarrassment for MI6, meant that the less anyone knew about it the better.'

'Plus, Morrison decided to cover his ass.'

'By denying it ever existed.'

This time it was Daisy who shook her head. 'And in so doing he made both you and me look like liars, Rupert.'

'Which also made us appear more guilty.'

Aidan was working out the timeline. 'So it seems to me Mildew came to see you, Rupert, then checked out what you said with Morrison, and then came to see us. *After* he'd been told you were talking bullshit. Which then made Daisy look even more suspicious when she told him the same story.'

'Morrison has dropped us both in it... and that's without Mildew knowing what we did after all that happened,' said Rupert.

'It's not looking good, my friend,' said Daisy quietly.

'No, it isn't. It was bad enough without including the two secret flights I'd arranged on your behalf in the last year. If Mildew gets to find out about those...'

Daisy put a hand on his arm. 'He *can't* find out, Rupert. If he does then we can both kiss goodbye to the rest of our lives.'

'But what can we do? Aidan's brother Charlie can verbally tell Mildew he built the tech, but he's out of the game now, and I would assume all of his documentary evidence went up when he burnt his farmhouse to the ground. Which if I remember right was down to you again, Daisy.'

'Guilty as charged. I was the one who fired the slug into the propane tank. *Rupert...*'

'Oh dear. I know that look.'

'I've been thinking.'

'Hell, please don't.'

'Just listen. All this hinges on the allegations of my treason back in ninety-eight. If we can prove to Mildew I wasn't a double agent after all then he'll have no case, and all the stuff from recent times will go away.'

'That's true. But how the hell do we prove something that didn't happen all that time ago?'

'I'm not sure. But what I am sure of is there's only one person who might hold a key to unlocking the facts from back then.'

'Surely not... Su Shi?'

Daisy nodded. 'It's a faint hope, Rupert, but I think it's the only one we've got.'

'Can you get in touch with her?'

'Our phones are bugged, and it's likely yours are too. But in reality, even if she came out of hiding to defend us, which for her sake mustn't happen, it's actual *documents* we need, not words. When we sealed her into that crate ready for the secret transport to Emerald Island you arranged, she had her large backpack with her. I think the documents she'd accumulated over twenty years may have been in that backpack. Documents that might possibly clear my name, and subsequently yours too.'

'Hell Daisy, that is for sure a long shot. Even if she's still got those documents there may not be anything there Mildew would take any notice of.'

'Yes, I know. And they're in the Caribbean as well, in the possession of someone who has apparently disappeared off the face of the Earth.'

'So even if they exist we can hardly get her to send us them by airmail.'

'Exactly. That's way too risky and would take too long anyway. We need to clip Mildew's wings right now, before he gets his teeth into you for impropriety.'

'So I assume you're intending going over there?'

'Um, yes... but there's a slight problem.'

'Go on.'

'Mildew has confiscated our passports. We can't go anywhere... not officially anyway.'

'*Daisy?* You can't be suggesting..?'

'We're in this together, Rupert. If we don't take this slim chance we're both getting banged up.'

'You *are* suggesting.'

'You've done it twice before. One more time won't make any difference, will it?'

Rupert threw his eyes to the ceiling. 'You know as well as me that's crap, Daisy. If we get caught now, that really is curtains.'

'So you won't help me... or yourself either then?'

'I... I didn't say that. It's just what you're asking...'

'Can you still make it happen?'

'Oh hell. I can, but...'

'But what, Rupert?'

'Oh boy... I play golf once a week at Elveden with the commander of the Mildenhall airbase. That's how I arranged it before. But...'

'When is your next session?'

'Tomorrow. I just...'

'For me, Rupert? And for your own skin, ultimately. And for old time's sake?'

'Daisy, you're impossible.'

'I know. Aidan says the same thing, don't you dear?'

He chuckled mirthlessly. 'Talking cricket bats again, Rupert, I think you're on a losing wicket.'

'Oh hell.'

'It will be hell if we don't pull this off. It's got to happen in the next few days, or Mildew will have managed to get his grubby hands around even more juicy morsels of assumed guilt.'

'I'm aware of that.'

'Then you will help?'

'Do I have a choice?'

'I can't see either of us do, no.'

'You're impossible.'

'You already said that.'

Chapter 9

'Cornwall?'

'It's for a friend. We met her while you were in Africa, Celia. She's got a bit of a problem right now, so your father and I said we'd go and help. It will only be for a few days.'

'I would have thought you had enough problems of your own right now.'

'Well we do, but they are kind of in the hands of Morbid Mildew. Edna needs us, so perhaps it will take our minds off our own issues.'

Aidan added to the argument. 'You know your mother... she'll always be there if a friend is in trouble.'

'Yes she would. But I still don't believe you.'

'Have I ever lied to you, dear?'

'Yes, a few times.'

Daisy looked away from her daughter's stare. 'Okay, but only when it was necessary.'

'Like now?'

'If that's what you wish to believe. I can't say any more because you'll just assume we'll be lying.'

'Mum...'

Aidan wrapped an arm around Celia's shoulder. 'Take no notice, Celia. Things seem to be piling up right now, so a few days away might help.'

'And what about us? What if Mildew turns up again, looking for you?'

'I'll leave you a can of mould remover,' said Daisy.

'That's not remotely funny.'

Aidan shook his head. 'She has a point, Flower. Acid remarks aren't what we need right now.'

Daisy wiped away a tear. 'I'm sorry, Celia. But on the actual Mildew front, the less you know the better.'

'So that when he uses the thumbscrews we can't tell him anything even if we wanted to?'

'Something like that, yes.'

Aidan gave his wife a disapproving stare. 'What Daisy means is that thumbscrews went out with the ark, and even if he did turn up he would ask you two where we were in a politically-correct way.'

'This is the SIS we're talking about, dad.'

'Yes, and they're currently having to be very careful with their tactics, which means you will be safe.'

'So you're not going to tell us where you're really going?' said Jack.

'Don't you start. I *did* tell you. Cornwall.'

'Okay. Point taken.'

'We have to go. We just called to let you know we'll be out of contact for a few days.'

'Out of contact? It's Cornwall, not the dark side of the moon.'

'Please just stop asking questions. Where we're going is in a mobile phone dead zone.'

Jack put a hand on Celia's arm. 'Leave it, baby. Neither of them is going to give.'

'We'll let you know when we're back,' said Daisy cheerily as she breezed out of the kitchen door.

The cheery breezing didn't last long. Daisy rubbed the gloss away from her eyes. 'I hate lying to them, Dip.'

'I know. But it's for their own good, dear. Celia's point about Mildew turning up is a good one. If he finds out where we've gone he'll put two and two together and make ninety-eight.'

'I assume that number wasn't just plucked out of the air, Dip?'

'Just making a point.'

'Point noted. I suppose we'd better go tell more lies to Sarah now.'

'Cornwall?'

'Yes. I've never told you about Edna, but we became friends before you came on the scene.'

'Really?'

'Is it that surprising I have friends?'

'Well, no. But...'

'Then stop looking so astonished, Sarah.'

'I wasn't. I'm just struggling to believe you right now.'

'Have I ever... okay, we just came to ask you to keep in touch with Celia and Jack while we're gone. Edna lives in a signal dead zone.'

'That's convenient.'

'Sarah? That's uncalled for.'

'And I do keep in touch with Celia anyway. So why are you asking me to do what you already know I will?'

'I... well...'

'Daisy is just worried Mildew might come snooping around while we're... in Cornwall. Celia and Jack might need some moral support.'

'So where are you really going?'

'Cornwall.'

'Okay. Just know that if I get a phone call asking me to join you, I'll refuse... I'm not ending up in a wheelchair again if you can't be truthful with me.'

'Just be there for Celia, please.'

'There won't be a call, Sarah. We'll be in a dead zone, remember?' said Aidan, still trying to add weight to the lies.

'Yeah, sure.'

'So why does no one believe us, Dip?'
'Maybe because they all know us too well.'
'Or I've got too old to be a convincing liar.'
'Perhaps that's no bad thing, Flower.'
'Right now it is. Oh well, let's go and face Maisie.'

'Cornwall?'
'Oh for god's sake. Why is it so unbelievable to want to go to Cornwall?'

Maisie shook her head. 'It's a long way from here, dear.'

'I'll go to the ends of the Earth to help a friend in need, Maisie.'

'I know. Or the bottom of the North Sea, all because of an uprooted rose bush.'

'We didn't make it to the bottom, thanks to our rescuers. And it actually wasn't for a plant, it was more to do with illegal drugs.'

Maisie smiled to Aidan, the way only she could. 'Don't worry, I know where you're going.'

'Um... you do?'

'I'm not an idiot. You're going to the Lake District.'

Daisy glanced to Aidan a little nervously. 'What makes you think that, Maisie?'

'That's where you went for that weekend with the local naturists last January, running around naked, indulging in drunken and debauched orgies... according what you told me after you got back anyway.'

'Ah... I see,' said Daisy with a sigh of relief.

'I knew Aidan had got a taste for the naturist life.'

'Excuse me?' said Aidan.

Daisy patted him on the shoulder, mostly to shut him up. 'Who'd believe it, hey? My husband is full of surprises.'

'Like the fact he's actually your husband... at the moment anyway.'

'Excuse me?' Aidan spluttered again.

'I've no plans to bin him, Maisie... not yet at least.'

'Excu...'

'Anyway, must dash. Lots of packing to do. We'll come and see you when we're back.'

'It was bad enough you telling Maisie I'm a closet naturist the first time round. Now she thinks it's a set-in-stone fact.'

'Just go with it, dear. If Mildew happens upon our dippy friend she'll be quite convincing about what we've gone to do... now you've bared your soul, as it were.'

'The things I do for you.'

'Daisy grinned. 'Maybe that should be the things you *are*, Dip... in some people's eyes anyway!'

'I give up.'

Chapter 10

The darkness of early morning was just beginning to fade as Daisy and Aidan packed two small cases into the boot of the BMW. Daisy shivered as the chill of the October morning penetrated her coat, but wasn't entirely sure it was just the external temperature.

Aidan noticed as she cast regretful eyes over the cottage. 'You okay, dear?'

She took his hand. 'Are we doing the right thing, Dip? There's only a remote chance Su Shi can help us after all.'

He opened the passenger door for her. 'I think it's the only available option left for us. At least a few days in the Caribbean might help us relax a little, if such a thing is possible right now.'

'You think I should have brought my crocheting kit?'

He let out a little laugh, but then realised she wasn't being entirely flippant. 'Maybe just a little tropical sun on a white sandy beach, Flower?'

She took his hand. 'It won't take away the fear of being thrown in the dungeons for treason when we get back, if our Chinese friend can't help us.'

'I know. We just have to keep the faith, dear.'

'I feel like a fugitive, reliant on the good nature of others to keep from being caught.'

'I think Rupert agrees with your assessment of Morbid Mildew digging up non-existent dirt. He's arranged the secret flight from Mildenhall to Venezuela after all, and someone to skipper us on a boat to Trinidad after that. It says a lot.'

Daisy nodded her head, Aidan's wise words hitting the spot she needed them to. 'I hope it's all worth it, dear.

We're even renting a car in Norwich so he can't trace the BMW driving to Mildenhall. Then there's god-knows how many hours in a military aircraft, followed by even more hours aboard a boat to Trinidad so Charlie can pick us up from there... and it might all be for nothing.'

'And he and Danielle don't even know we're coming until we get close.'

'We can't risk calling him from here, for his sake as well as ours, even though his only communication is via satellite. We've no idea how deep Mildew's snooping goes. For all we know there's a hidden camera in our toilet pan.'

Aidan chuckled. 'Thanks dear... that's a perfect image to set me off on our journey.'

'You love me really, you know you do.'

The staff had just turned up for their day's work at the car rental premises on Norwich's inner ring road as Daisy and Aidan arrived. The man with the keys looked a little puzzled they were swapping a smart BMW for a Kia compact, but Aidan explained it wasn't as reliable as it used to be, so he nodded and showed him where to store their car.

An hour and a half later they were driving through the somewhat-familiar gateway of Mildenhall airbase, and heading for the commander's office. He shook both their hands, and told them the C-130 was departing for Cumaná in Venezuela in an hour. He also told them his counterpart at the Venezuelan base had organised a private boat for the final leg to Trinidad, but cautioned them they'd had to arrange what they could at short notice.

'So we're not cruising in a luxury floating palace then, commander?'

'Um, hell no. This is the US military, Daisy. We were lucky enough that Hernandez was available.'

Aidan shook his head. 'Oh dear. Even his name sends a shiver down my spine.'

'Don't worry. He and his boat might be a little rough around the edges, but we've used him for covert operations before. Just ignore it if you see a dead Great White in the hold.'

Daisy shook her head, her eyes giving away the more-than-slight concern in her heart. 'What have we let ourselves in for, Dip?'

The flight in the C-130 transport wasn't so bad. Apart from a couple of Hummers in the cargo hold the aircraft was empty, and just a skeleton crew was onboard for the flight out. Daisy and Aidan were given half-comfortable seats at the rear of the cockpit, normally reserved for extra crew members.

It *wasn't* so bad, until the navigator filled them with dread. 'There's a hurricane currently spinning around the Venezuelan mainland, so we're heading on a flight path a little further north than usual. Don't worry though, it's dissipating now.'

'Um... which direction is it heading?' said Aidan in a small voice.

'North. But there's no problem, we'll be landed before it reaches Cumaná. It might even be all but done by then.'

Daisy swallowed hard, doing her best not to let the crew know she had. *'It's not the flight that worries me,'* she whispered to Aidan. *'A leaky old poaching boat doesn't sound like the ideal transport right now.'*

Daisy's nervous apprehension appeared to be justified as they stood next to the harbour walls that had seen better days, their reluctant eyes panning over their only means of transport for the final leg of their journey.

The Spanish wooden ex-fishing boat must have been fifty years old. Now enjoying a new lease of old age as a poaching boat, it looked to have more paint peeling from its hull than what was actually attached. The ancient superstructure was even tattier.

A small enclosed wheelhouse sat behind an equally-small forward cabin. The rear deck area was also the roof of an aft cabin, which looked like it must have been converted from part of the fish hold when the boat took on its new maritime role. A tiny fibreglass dinghy swung on davits over the stern. Daisy commented on the obvious.

'That dinghy isn't big enough for three, dear. Maybe we should draw straws now?'

He chuckled, doing his best to make light of a very dark situation. 'I'm sure if it came to it Hernandez would save his paying customers first, Flower.'

'Um... you are referring to *that* Hernandez?'

A slightly overweight man with shoulder-length black hair appeared from the wheelhouse and waved to them from the rear deck. *'Hey, gringos... you my vict... um, my passengers?'*

Aidan called back, his voice a little shaky. 'You Hernandez?'

'Sure thing. Captain Hernandez Garcia at your service. Come aboard my luxury liner.'

Daisy and Aidan stepped aboard what certainly wasn't a luxury liner, a little gingerly. Daisy looked their captain up and down, dressed as he was in his official passenger greeting uniform of flowered Caribbean shirt and dark red shorts. He did sport a captain's hat on his head though, which wasn't the slightest bit encouraging.

'I was under the impression Hernandez was a surname.'

He grinned, in a sickly kind of way. 'My momma and papa, they wanted me to have a name that meant something. So I am Hernandez!'

'What does it actually mean?'

'Adventurous.'

Aidan shook his head. 'Hmm... you might have to live up to your name if that hurricane is still around.'

He batted a dismissive hand across his mustached face. 'Nah... look, it is beautiful sunny evening now. We have radar too, so we can see what is coming.'

'All mod cons, hey?'

'You better believe it.'

'Why does this boat smell fishy?'

'It a working boat, lady. I catch fish that fetch good bolivars, see?'

'Hmm... as long as you don't get caught, hey?'

He changed the subject hastily. 'Talking of money, you got your fare? This liner it go nowhere until passengers pay up.'

Aidan pulled out his fattened wallet. 'Oh, you mean the extortionate ransom we're being charged for a third class cruise?'

'Hey... you folks is desperate, so I hear. Take it or leave it...'

Aidan handed him the wad, after a pleading look from his wife. 'US dollars, I'm afraid, Hernandez.'

'It okay... they good around here.'

'How long before we leave?'

'Now you have paid your passage, we go straightaway. Light is fading, and it is twelve-hour sightseeing cruise, so we depart, yes?'

'Sightseeing? In the dark?'

'You want to go or not?'

Daisy and Aidan sighed as one, and answered nervously as one too. 'Yes, unfortunately we do.'

Chapter 11

The boat began to vibrate in a slightly-worrying way. The engines had coughed and spluttered their way to life in a cloud of black diesel fumes, and Hernandez the poacher deftly flicked the mooring ropes looping around the bollards on the pontoon.

The boat moved slowly out into the harbour, and suddenly dry land was a thing of the past.

Then, as they headed out and turned to starboard into the Caribbean Sea , it shuddered a complaint as it hit a wave. They were leaving the shelter of the calm waters of the little bay. Within minutes they were passing through the straits between the mainland and the island of Porlamar. As they reached truly open water, a moment of slightly-increased fear welled over Daisy as she stood with Aidan on the rear deck. A wave tried to well over her too, bigger this time. Then the wind joined in, a bitter damp salty breeze that carried spray over them like an unwelcome cold shower.

'Best just chill out,' said Aidan, and then realised what a bad choice of phrase it was as he noticed Daisy shiver. She glanced to him, but there was none of the witty sarcasm usually present in her tone.

'Let's go into the cabin, Dip,' she said quietly as she took his hand. 'This is bringing back bad memories, and considering we're in the Caribbean it feels like winter anyway.'

'Yes, and it does seem to be getting a little choppy, dear.'

The boat was heading north-east into seriously open water, and as they joined Hernandez working hard at the helm he glanced to the radar and looked round. *'Hey crewmates, we might be in for a rough one. Hope you not seasick all over my pristine boat.'*

Daisy nodded slowly. 'Is it always this cold in Venezuela? I didn't bring a Parka.'

He grinned. 'Hey lady, you should be used to it in England. But sure, it is unusually cold for the time of year. In the forward cabin there is a couple of jumpers. One of them might stop you freezing to death!'

Daisy disappeared, and then reemerged from the cabin three minutes later, climbing the three steps into the wheelhouse, looking a little different.

'Wow... nice outfit!' Aidan grinned.

'OK, less of the sarcasm.' She'd slipped into a fisherman's-style jumper about fifty sizes too big, and found a pair of pink wellington boots for her feet. And just to lighten the mood, a bright yellow lifeboat-man's helmet.

'Well, at least if I have to go batten down the hatches, I'm ready for it.' She shook her helmeted head, the nervous dread in her stomach getting stronger, despite the slightly-comical appearance.

Aidan tried to lift her mood. 'Where the hell did you find pink wellies on a poaching boat, dear?'

Hernandez let out a kind of sarcastic snort. 'They belonged to my wife.'

'Oh, she... she's not with us anymore?'

'She not with me, for sure. Buggered off with a corrupt politician from Bolivia.'

'I'm sorry.'

He snorted again, and threw an expressive hand in the air. 'Me not. *Güebón muchacha.*'

'I take it that's not very complimentary?' said Aidan, glancing to his wife.

'My Venezuelan Spanish isn't that hot, but judging by his downturned mouth I don't think he was calling her a beautiful soul,' said Daisy.

Five minutes later all land was gone. The only thing in view was the Caribbean Sea, its increasing swell not exactly the perfect image of a tropical paradise. Daisy had to grab hold of a bulkhead to keep herself upright as a big wave hit the boat side on. 'We really shouldn't have come in October, Dip,' she said, the slight shake in her voice not difficult to detect.

Aidan grinned, but it was hard to see any mirth within the smile. The boat shuddered again, and Daisy glanced through the big windows at the dark ocean, even though she couldn't really see further than a hundred metres.

They could no longer see where the angry sea ended and the dark sky started.

'Did you say a *little choppy*? How much of this do we have to take?'

'It about twelve hours to Trinidad,' said Hernandez, starting to look a little green around the edges. 'You should get some sleep.'

'Sleep? On this roller coaster?'

'Okay, sure. Whatever you want.'

Daisy glanced to Aidan. 'Is it my imagination, or does our captain look scared out of his wits?'

'He does look a little worried, dear.'

Aidan wobbled his way over to the radar screen fixed above the instrument panel, and studied the image. 'Yep, there's a bit of a storm ahead.'

Daisy leant her chin on his shoulder as she narrowed her eyes at the image. Then she screwed up her face.

'You always were a master of understatement, Dip.'

Daisy and Aidan decided watching the radar screen was just too depressing, so headed to the galley to tip some dried pasta and sauce packet meals into a saucepan for the three of them. Two minutes later they heard a shout from the bridge. Aidan went to see what Hernandez wanted. As he struggled up the steps in the pitching boat, the captain asked if he could be relieved for a comfort break. There had to be hands on the wheel at all times, the waves ready to whip the rudder around at any moment if it was left unattended.

Aidan nodded, and called back down to let Daisy know he was the temporary helmsman. They were several miles off the coast, and the storm was building relentlessly. Hernandez disappeared into the rear cabin, and Aidan sucked in a deep breath to help him concentrate more on keeping the boat on its correct heading, rather than the fact it was getting increasingly difficult to do so.

Five minutes later Daisy appeared, with two bowls of steaming pasta in her hands.

'You still wearing that silly hat?'

'No, I just put it on to make you smile when I come up here. Don't you think I look sexy?' she laughed, taking it off and putting it on Aidan's head instead. Her actions weren't hiding the apprehension... and he knew her well enough to recognise her *brave face,* which took the form of silly humour that was intended to raise the mood.

For herself, as much as for anyone else.

'Where's our captain?' she asked. 'His food will be getting cold.'

'He went into his cabin under the rear deck. Not seen him for ten minutes. Give him a shout.'

Daisy turned to make her way to the rear of the boat, but then saw something that welded her feet to the wooden bridge floor. *'Aidan...'* she gasped.

He glanced around in horror at the urgency in her voice. It was well founded.

'Oh no...'

Chapter 12

They just managed to reach the stern of the deck as Hernandez was letting go of the dinghy's ropes. As Aidan shouted out the outboard motor fired up, and the tiny boat began to move away.

The wind and the spray made hearing anything difficult, but as Hernandez and the dinghy disappeared into the darkness, it sounded like, *'You'll be okay, my friends. I think. Farewell, and good luck...'*

Daisy let out a little sob. 'The slimy little Spanish toad.'

Aidan grabbed her hand. 'He obviously saw something that made him decide to jump ship, which he then did from that rear hatch so we wouldn't see him.'

'With our extortionate fare in his pocket.'

'I think we'd better get inside, and take the wheel.'

Back at the controls, Aidan studied the radar screen. He hitched a fearful breath, and gave Daisy the news. 'I don't want to worry you even more, but take a look at this... it was clearly the reason our captain deserted.' He pointed to the swirl of grey circling the boat's position.

Daisy looked at him in horror, realising straightaway what he'd seen. 'That looks suspiciously like the hurricane they said might be heading our way.'

He nodded. 'Yes, although from what the US airmen said, it was dissipating.'

'Stop being so positive. It doesn't look dissipated to me, and this unexpected cold and the stormy sea tends to confirm it.'

'It could be worse. If this wasn't just the remnants of hurricane Madeline we'd likely not be here now.'

'Please don't sweeten this, dear. Hermandez obviously didn't want to stick around to take the risk.'

Aidan panned out the image. 'It looks like the north shore of Venezuela is about six miles south. That's obviously where our cowardly captain is scuttling to. Maybe we should head the same way.'

'So why didn't he just turn the boat for the shore?'

'The outboard on that dinghy was a powerful one. I think maybe he used it because it was a lot faster than this old tub.'

'Dear, think about it. He risked a dangerous journey in a silly little boat... maybe because he knows these waters and realised it was the only way to survive?'

'You do have a way with words, Flower.'

'You mean I tend to point out the harsh truth?'

'Perhaps. I suppose following him is just as bad an option as keeping to our easterly course.'

'Now who's got a way with words?'

'Let's just stick it out. Despite how it looks, the remnants of this hurricane might be done in an hour or so.'

Aidan spent a half-hour struggling with the wheel until Daisy took over, telling him to go grab an hour or two of sleep before his next stint. He looked exhausted. A long flight followed by a fraught sea voyage meant that a little rest was essential.

He'd been curled up in the cabin for an hour when the heart of the storm found them, in a way impossible to ignore.

The mast on the foredeck came crashing down.

It wasn't a big mast, fortunately. Designed to carry a small sail used as a get-you-home facility if the engines failed, it was still heavy enough to make a huge noise as it hit the wheelhouse roof.

Daisy, at the helm, shrieked and covered her face as it fell towards her, but nothing else broke. It seemed only seconds before Aidan was in the wheelhouse.

'What happened...*oh shit...*' Straightaway he saw the mast swinging around the cabin roof, still attached to the ropes that until a few moments ago had held it upright.

'I've got to cut it free, Daisy... it'll do damage if we leave it. If it starts dragging in the sea it could have us over.'

'*You can't go on deck in this!*' she shouted, struggling to keep the wheel steady.

'Got no choice... I'll have to rope myself to something.' Aidan was foraging around in the lockers beneath the seats as he spoke. 'This will do.'

He pulled out a coil of sturdy rope. 'I need a sharp knife.' He disappeared into the cabin. Daisy heard the cutlery draw crashing to the ground.

'Got one.' He climbed back into the wheelhouse with a serrated kitchen knife, and looked desperately through the windows to try and work out how he was going to cut the mast free without drowning himself.

'There's a roof hatch in the little cabin in the bows. That will get you nearer,' Daisy said. Just as she spoke, another of the ropes holding the mast snapped, and it rolled from the roof onto the starboard deck.

'It would have been a good idea until that just happened, dear.' Aidan replied, looking a little rueful, as well as a lot more scared out of his wits. 'Now I'll have to get on the side deck and cut it free from there.' He threw on a life jacket as he spoke.

'*Aidan...*'

'I'll be ok, Daisy.'

'You'd better be... it's your turn at the wheel.'

Aidan was uncoiling the rope. 'Flower, you'll have to let go of the wheel for a minute. Tie this around me as tight as you can.' He already had a loose loop around him, so she let go of the wheel and tied far more knots than she really needed to.

'Dear, I need to breathe, you know.'

'You're not getting away from me now,' she retorted, a little unconvincingly.

'Ok, slow the engines, and try and keep the boat pointing into the waves. If we get a sidewinder I'll be gone.'

'Please don't say that.'

Daisy grabbed the wheel again, as Aidan opened the rear doors. The full force of the storm blasted around them in an instant. The thickly-glazed windows had kept much of the noise at bay, but with the doors open there was nothing between them and the elements.

Aidan looked a little taken aback for a moment, but then he staggered out onto the rear deck, searching desperately for something to rope himself to. The handrails on the wheelhouse roof were big and chunky, so he decided they would have to do. The bitter cold of the spray numbed his fingers in an instant, but he managed to tie the rope around the rail.

Just as he was about to pull on it to test its strength, the boat hit a huge wave and crashed back down at an angle. He grasped the rope desperately as Daisy screamed in fear, knowing if he'd been a few seconds later tying it he would have been pitched into the sea.

The wild spray was everywhere, so cold it was beginning to build up on the deck, almost like snow. Aidan's half-frozen face set itself into a grim expression, as he realised the freezing spray was about to make his job even more difficult.

He could almost touch the top of the mast straight away, but that wasn't where he needed to be. Further forward, the base of the mast had broken from the deck and was dangling over the side of the boat, kept in place by the ropes still attached to the sides of the hull. There was no option but to work his way along the deck, already partly blocked by the mast, so he could get to the ropes and cut them. He started to ease himself forward. Daisy watched from the relative safety of the wheelhouse, her hands white-knuckling the wheel that seemed to have a mind of its own.

She knew as well as he that Aidan's task wouldn't have been the easiest at the best of times, let alone in a force eight.

He slipped on the spray covering the deck, but the rope did its job. She saw him glance to her through the wheelhouse windows. For his sake she kept the look of sheer terror off her face, fighting to keep the boat pointing into the wind and smile to him at the same time. He gave her a thumbs-up, both of them knowing it was a bit of an unspoken lie.

His feet were in the tiny space between the mast and the cabin side. He was close to reaching the first of the ropes. The part of the mast hanging over the side was yawing constantly, and once he started cutting ropes it was anyone's guess how it would react.

He sawed through the first rope. The mast stayed where it was. *Three more to go, each one trickier than the last.* He inched forward, so much spray on the deck he had virtually no grip at his feet. The spray hitting him was turning him white, as it froze into salty snow in mid air.

Somehow he reached the next two ropes and began cutting. One more rope was gone, but then the base of the mast began to drag in the waves, changing the angle of the rest of the mast so it was pressing his feet against the cabin side, stopping him from moving any further.

Aidan managed to reach out to the third rope, and began sawing. He couldn't feel his hands anymore, relying on sight only, but even that was difficult. The freezing spray was building up on his eyelids, and he didn't have a spare hand to wipe it away.

The third rope was cut. Then his world went crazy. Everything happened in a single second. The base of the mast tipped into the sea, the drag of the water breaking the last rope as if it was cotton. The mast finally broke clear of the boat, and crashed into the sea.

As it did so, it took Aidan with it.

Chapter 13

'Aidan!' Daisy screamed frantically as he suddenly disappeared from her view. She wrenched the throttles closed and ran out onto the rear deck, not realising how slippery it was. Grabbing crazily for a deck rail as she fell, one hand stopped her from going over the stern. She drew in a deep salt-laden breath to calm herself, and struggled back closer to the wheelhouse doors.

She could see the mast floating away in the rough seas, but there was no sign of Aidan. He wasn't anywhere on the deck either. Sheer terror tried to turn her to a weeping statue, but then she heard a muffled, frantic cry.

'Daisy… help me please…'

Somehow she dragged herself to the side of the rear deck and hung her head over the edge of the hull.

'Flower… down here.' He was almost fully submerged in the water, clinging on to a fender, and still attached to his rope.

'Wait there…' she cried, fighting her way back into the wheelhouse, and wondering if it was her imagination or if he really did say *'like I'm going anywhere'*. She grabbed a lifebelt with a length of rope attached to it, ran back onto the deck, and lowered it to Aidan.

'Try and get this over your head… I'll pull you up.'

'You'll never pull me up.'

'Just shut up and do it!'

He managed to loop it over one shoulder, but his safety rope was in the way of getting it any further around him.

'Ok, that'll have to do,' Daisy shouted. 'You pull up on your end and I'll pull mine.'

'I can't feel my hands… or anything else.'

A dull ache of desperation thudded into Daisy's stomach. He was starting to sound weaker, the arctic wind and the lashing rain not helping. If she didn't get him back on the deck right then she wouldn't get him back at all.

She wrapped her legs around a deck stanchion and started to pull. Aidan didn't seem able to do much to help, but she found it easier than she thought, and a few seconds later his head appeared above the deck.

'Come on... grab the rail!'

'I can't move.'

'Yes you can, Moby... hook your arm over it.'

He managed to loop his arm around the rail. She grabbed him roughly by his lifejacket and heaved him onto the deck. With no one at the helm the boat was slewing in all directions. Capsizing was a very real possibility, but Aidan was all but immobilised, clinging onto the safety rail without the strength to go any further. Somehow she had to get them both back into the cabin.

She had an idea. He still had the lifebuoy half around him.

'Aidan!' She screamed, realising he was losing consciousness. 'Aidan... try and hang on to the deck rail. I'm going into the wheelhouse, and then I'll pull you in after me. Don't let go of the life-ring!'

She waited a moment that seemed like an eternity until the boat topped the crest of a wave and was pointing back down, then let go of the deck rail and almost slid back into the wheelhouse. Even before she hit something to stop the slide, she'd started to pull Aidan in with the lifebuoy rope.

'Come on you big lump... talk about a stranded whale...'

Then, almost before she knew it, he was inside with her. She ran to the doors and used her momentum to shut away the nightmare outside. Seconds later she was on the floor beside him, pulling him close. He was freezing, but there was no time to hold him, the boat still being thrown in all directions.

She struggled to her feet and opened the throttles to give the boat some steering way, then brought it round back on course. Wrenching the lifebuoy off Aidan, she used the rope to tie the wheel in place to stop it spinning round. Flicking the heater switch, she turned it up to full.

Ripping the sodden clothes off him, she bundled his semi-conscious body into the aft cabin where there were some dry towels and thick blankets, and gave him a brisk rubbing down. He glanced up to her with eyes that still wouldn't focus, and when he forced out words it sounded like he was drunk.

'How did you do that?'

'Do what?'

'Pull me out of the water?'

'You almost died... *again*... and all you can think about is how I managed to pull you out? I'm stronger than I look, okay?'

'Sorry.'

'Just warm up or you *will* die.' She smothered him in the blankets. 'I'm going to put the kettle on, make us some soup.'

'Sounds like the best idea ever.'

Chapter 14

An hour later, things were looking better. Aidan was warming up nicely, three mugs of chicken soup helping his temperature along, and the vicious storm had started to abate. The motion of the boat was smoother, and they could move around without having to hang on to every available support.

Aidan had just taken over helm duties, despite Daisy's protests, telling her he could warm up just as well at the wheel as he could on the sofa. He beckoned her over.

'Look, Daisy.'

'What?'

He pointed to the radar screen. 'The storm is disappearing.'

She glanced out of the side window. 'It's getting light... look.' Through the windscreen they could make out the edge of the ocean, dark against the lightening sky behind it. The end of the Venezuelan peninsula was disappearing behind them. It was time to turn south, and head for the western coast of Trinidad. Aidan looked at his watch. It was seven o'clock. They'd been at sea for twelve hours, and it wouldn't be too long before they would see the rocky coastline of their destination.

An hour and a half later it was fully light, and they'd found the coast. They cruised the boat further south, keeping a couple of miles offshore, using the coastline as a guide to take them to somewhere on the shore south of Port of Spain. There they could make land as close to Emerald Island as Trinidad got, without anyone knowing they were there.

In complete contrast to the dramatic night the sea was like a millpond, and a morning sun beamed strongly through the Caribbean air. Other than their broken boat and the lack of a captain, there was no indication of the hell they'd been through a few hours earlier.

Daisy braved the rear deck, wearing her lifeboat-man's hat and pink boots. Then her face broke into a beautiful smile, as it finally sunk in their current reality was far nicer than their previously stormy one.

'Come on Aidan, get your shorts on... it's lovely out here!'

'I'll wear mine if you wear yours,' he grinned.

'Ok, point taken.' She came back in. It was still chilly after all. 'I think it's time for you to call Charlie and Danielle on their satellite connection, and give them the shock of their lives.'

'Aidan? Good to hear from you, Bro... and the connection is better than normal.'

'That's because we're in the Caribbean, on our way to come and see you.'

'What? Why didn't you warn us... I mean, give us time to prepare?'

'Um... it's complicated. We'll explain when we're face-to-face.'

'You want us to pick you up from Port of Spain?'

'Well, um... a little further south than that. We're kind of not supposed to be away from home, and we don't want anyone finding out we're here.'

The voice hesitated. *'Ade... what's going on?'*

'As I said, face-to-face. We're currently on an old fishing boat cruising south along Trinidad's west coast, on our way to find a quiet beach so we can sneak onto land that way. Thanks, Charlie.'

'I can't wait to hear this story. Sounds like the old days of MI6. It'll take us three hours or so to reach you guys though. You'll have to let us know exactly where you are.'

'Will do, once we make land, which should be in the next hour.'

'Can't wait. Ade... are you and Daisy okay?'

'Physically yes, apart from almost getting shipwrecked. But... well, something's going down, and we need your help.'

'Face-to-face yeah?'

'Call you when we hit solid ground.'

Aidan's words were nearer to the mark than he realised. As he killed the call he noticed their next little problem. The fuel tanks were almost empty. He pointed out the gauges to Daisy.

'Better head for shore then, Dip. We've just passed Port of Spain, and according to the map there's lots of secluded coves where we won't need a passport.'

Aidan spun the wheel to port. 'The sooner the better, I think.'

Fifteen minutes later, half a mile offshore, one of the fuel tank warning lights started flashing. They both knew it would only be minutes before the second one would be empty too.

'Time to make solid ground I think,' said Daisy.

Aidan was scanning a small deserted cove in the distance. 'There... but there's no such thing as a landing stage.'

'It'll have to be the beach then.'

'Huh?'

'Hernandez was kind enough to gift us his boat. Quite frankly when Charlie and Danielle get here we really have no need for it.'

'You mean..?'

'Once we get into shallow water, stick the engines on full. The momentum should carry us onto the beach, so with a bit of luck we won't even need to get our feet wet.'

'That assumes there's enough fuel left. And once the propellers hit the ground they'll wreck the bottom of the hull.'

'And your point is?'

'I guess I don't really have one.'

Daisy grinned, and wrenched the throttles to full. Aidan gritted his teeth as the old boat headed rapidly for the beach. Just before it met the sand of the shallows, the engines began to stutter. It didn't make any difference... five seconds later an expensive-sounding crunch filled their ears, as the props ran out of water and shattered as the sand ripped the blades away and sent them through the bottom of the hull.

That didn't matter either. The heavy old boat came to a shuddering stop twenty feet clear of the water, and then, like a Disney cartoon, ever-so-slowly tipped over to a thirty-degree angle.

'Come on, Captain Mickey... time to get off before we slide off!' said Daisy.

'Right behind you, Minnie,' said Aidan, as he reached for their travel cases.

'Why did you grab a duvet?' Aidan wheezed as they headed quickly up the beach to the tree line.

Daisy sank onto the soft sand with a huge sigh of relief. 'It's going to take Charlie three hours to get here, so before we do anything else we're going to take time out and get some sleep... together this time.'

'We mustn't be too long.'

'So the sooner we get into bed the sooner we can get up again! Call your brother and tell him where we are, and then shuggle up with me...'

Aidan grinned, and called Charlie to tell them to look out for a beached fishing boat five miles south of the town. Ignoring his gasp of astonishment he killed the call, and sixty seconds later they were in each other's arms under the duvet. Almost instantly Daisy felt herself drifting away, but she managed to speak softly to Aidan while she was still conscious enough to get words out.

'What a day, huh? Almost drowned... again... and on the run like fugitives who don't even know if they can prove their innocence ... what else lies ahead, Dip?'

'I haven't a clue, dear... but I do know you've been an absolute star, and you don't deserve any of this.'

She tried to give him a playful punch, but was so tired it ended up being more of a gentle brush of hand against arm. 'You will look after me, won't you?' she whispered, almost asleep.

He looked into her just-open eyes, and knew how vulnerable she was feeling. 'Quite honestly it seems just lately it's you looking after me. But we will always be there for each other, come what may.'

'Always. When I saw you hanging off the boat in that storm I knew I wouldn't have a clue what to do without you.'

'Guess that makes two of us then. I love you.'

She didn't reply. He could feel her warm breath against the hand she'd pressed to her face, and knew she'd drifted into sleep.

For a minute or two Aidan held her tight against him. Both of them, conscious or otherwise, were desperate to cling onto the brief moment of comfort their situation could easily take away. Then he felt his eyes getting too heavy to keep open and fell into a deep sleep, tightly spooning his exhausted wife.

Chapter 15

'Well, this is a sight I never thought I'd see.'
Daisy sat bolt upright, rubbing her eyes to dispel the unconsciousness. *'Danielle?* Oh gosh, I didn't think we'd be asleep this long,' she slurred.

Aidan scrambled out from under the duvet, staggering to get himself upright, until his brother caught him. 'Great to see you, Ade. It's a good job you told us to look out for a beached fishing trawler though, 'cause we'd never had thought to search for two old fogies snuggled up under a duvet in a secluded cove.'

'Hey, less of the old fogies,' said Aidan, stretching his aching back to not exactly disprove Charlie's words. 'Okay, mute point taken.'

Danielle glanced back to the wrecked boat. 'Couldn't find a landing stage, huh? Typical Daisy move.'

Daisy grinned, slightly sheepishly. 'Excuse me? We were out of gas, so we didn't have a lot of choice.'

'Bet you enjoyed ramming the beach though.'
'Well...'

Charlie looked like he was itching to know the gory details. 'I guess you caught the tail of hurricane Madeline? Dying to know all about the fun and games, but we'd better get gone. We're only five miles from Port of Spain, and although the hurricane kept people indoors it's gone now, so we might have company soon. Tell all on the way.'

Daisy and Aidan told all on the way. Huddled together in the wheelhouse of the small fast cruiser, Charlie and Danielle alternatively raised their eyebrows and shook their heads as each gory detail emerged. Then Charlie gave one final shake of his head.

'Seems to me if I wasn't off the grid the delightful Eric Mildew would have been shining a bright light into my face too.'

'Trust me, you guys are in the best place right now.'

'I'm not sure Su Shi can do anything to help you, but at least you can have a few days away from persecution,' said Danielle ruefully.

'We're glad to be here, however it turns out,' said Daisy.

'*Really* glad,' added Aidan.

'How is Su Shi getting on?'

'Very well. We've just about finished the refurb of the lodge, although we haven't seen her for a couple of days. Most of the time we leave her to her own devices, except when we're helping her bring the place up to scratch.'

'And Willy?'

'Oh, he's a changed man... um, AI. He's dedicated himself to the monkey school.'

'The what?'

Charlie chuckled. 'We were sceptical when he first told us he wanted to teach the local monkeys to be more intelligent, but incredibly he's stuck at it, and so have they. He even built a schoolhouse at the back of his shack. Right now he's preparing diplomas for his best pupils.'

'And I thought Daisy being accused of treason was out of this world,' said Aidan disbelievingly.

'This is Emerald Island,' Danielle grinned.

'And we are all supposedly descended from simians.'

Daisy giggled. 'That may be so, but I think Willy has stolen your title of the Wizard of Oz, Charlie.'

'I think it's safe to say he's found the end of his rainbow.'

The artificially-intelligent Willy caught the mooring ropes as the small cruiser edged against the landing stage on the eastern side of Emerald Island. As he tied them to the bollards and everyone climbed out, Daisy looked him up and down. 'Well Willy, you look different.'

He smiled warmly. 'Yes, Daisy. It's a shame I don't tan, otherwise I'd be even more different.'

'You don't look so much like a scarecrow anymore.'

'Thanks to Danielle and Su Shi. They made me better hands and feet and got rid of my straw hair, despite the original efforts of my maker here, who originally insisted I look exactly like a scarecrow.'

'It was necessary at the time, Willy. I did make you on a farm, and you were a secret project, so you had to blend in,' said Charlie, likely not for the first time.

'So how are you doing, Willy?' asked Aidan.

'Top of the tree, thanks. Although lately I seem to be getting the occasional urge to burn official documents... for some odd reason.'

Aidan chuckled. 'I guess old habits die hard.'

'Hmm... I'm trying to distance myself from the ex-president whose character I inherited, but he doesn't seem to want to go away completely.'

Danielle indicated the old colonial house a couple of hundred yards away. 'Let's go and settle you two in, and sort out some island food. You look like you could do with it.'

'Yes... bananas only go so far.'

'Madeline doesn't seem to have done too much damage here, Charlie.'

'Just a few trees uprooted, but we've got too many of those anyway. It's the hurricane season here, so we were kind of prepared for it... as much as you can be anyway.'

'Luckily it was weakening when it hit here,' said Danielle.

'Really?' said Aidan, trying not to, but unable to stop recalling the freezing water lashing around his helpless body.

'I don't want to put a dampener on things, Aidan, but if it had been full-strength you wouldn't be sitting here now. Sorry.'

Aidan found a grin, somehow. 'I was damp enough, thank you all the same.'

Charlie decided it might be best to change the subject. 'So you think Su Shi might have some sort of records that could exonerate you?'

Daisy lowered her eyes. 'I know it's last chance saloon, but she did have a large backpack with her when we packed her into that crate for the secret journey to here.'

Charlie put a hand on her arm. 'I wish I could help, but I wasn't personally involved back then. And I didn't even know where the surveillance tech I designed in later years had been located.'

'It's okay Charlie, we know you can't assist with this, and even if you could we wouldn't do anything to give away your location. That's why we almost lost our lives getting here by means of deserting skippers and a rickety old fishing boat.'

'Yes, and if Su Shi can help, it's even more important we don't give away where *she* is in the process,' added Aidan.

'For sure. It would rather ruin all your hard work in getting her here without anyone except Rupert knowing.'

Daisy looked even more down. 'In a way that's another thing worrying me. If Morbid Mildew gets his teeth into Rupert he might let stuff out to save his own skin.'

'I don't think he'd do that,' said Charlie.

'Neither do I. It would leave him open to even more retribution if MI6 knew he'd done things after his retirement that he really shouldn't.'

'Just hang onto that, Daisy. It's almost dark now, but first thing tomorrow after you've had a proper night's rest we'll go see Su Shi. Let's hope she still has a magic bullet.'

'She always hated guns. The sword was her weapon of choice.'

'Okay then... let's hope she can slice Mildew's witch hunt into microscopic and useless pieces.'

Chapter 16

'So guys, where does all this electricity come from on what is basically a desert island with too many trees?' asked Aidan at the breakfast table.

Charlie pointed through the big windows to a small building a hundred yards away. 'The guy who gifted me the island after he died lived here for years with his small family. Being English, he made sure he had all the home comforts he needed. That shed houses a huge diesel generator. It's ancient and uses a scary amount of fuel, but it still works, and supplies power to this place and Su Shi's lodge half a mile away.'

'But the satellite communications you guys use weren't invented in those days?' said Daisy.

'No, but he built a communications mast so they could keep in touch with the mainland via radio. I just modified it for today's world... after a few trips to Trinidad for some tech I had shipped over.'

'Lucky you're so handy in that department, Bro,' said Aidan.

Charlie smiled ruefully. 'We wanted the minimum of contact with the outside world, but we had to have some way of keeping in touch with you guys, and Stonewall and Weeney of course.'

'Weeney?' Daisy chuckled.

Danielle giggled with her. 'I'm afraid Stonewall's play on names kind of stuck. Even she likes it now.'

'You see much of them?'

'They were here last weekend, helping with Su Shi's place. There was still a lot to do, and undergrowth to clear away. They're back in Los Angeles this week.'

'I guess Stonewall is making another four movies all at once?' said Daisy.

'Something like that. He says he needs to give his adoring fans as much as he can before he gets cast aside for the next action hero.'

'Hmm... he's likely right about that.'

Danielle carried the empty plates to the butler sink. 'We should go see Su Shi. We've not heard from her for three days, but you guys need to find out if she's got anything to help you anyway.'

'Is it unusual to not see her for that long?'

Charlie shook his head. 'It's not unheard of, but we normally make sure we meet up every two days, especially with the refurb of the lodge.'

Aidan rose to his still-weary feet. 'Let's go. The sooner we know the better or the worst for Daisy, the sooner we can either raise a glass or cry into something alcoholic.'

The four of them took the well-trodden path to the old lodge that was once the home of the previous owner's daughter and her husband. Like the main house, it was situated on the southern shore of the tiny island. The north shore was rockier and less hospitable, so the English gent had based his family on the south side of the tiny island, which more resembled everyone's idea of a tropical paradise.

Aidan let out a low whistle as the house came into view. 'Wow... this is a *lodge*?'

Charlie smiled, slightly ruefully. 'As I said, the previous owner's long-dead parents made their fortune from a sugar cane trade staffed by slaves. He didn't approve, but inherited their wealth anyway. It had already built the main house and the lodge, fortunately for us to a high English standard.'

'It looks like a west-London folly.'

Danielle laughed. 'If it was in Kensington it would be worth a small fortune in its own right.'

The lodge was built of painted wood, but the design was just about as English as English got. Two storeys high, the first floor had been incorporated into a tall steeply-sloping red-tiled roof, with dormer windows to give natural light to the bedrooms. Each had its own pitched roof, and consisted of elegant round-topped double doors opening onto small balconies. All three boasted stunning views of the ocean.

In the centre of the front wall, a pillastered neo-classical entrance would have graced the face of the Bank of England building. Floor to ceiling windows either side of it consisted of more double doors opening out onto a three-sided flagstone terrace, traversing the front and both sides of the house.

Slightly-mouldy wired glass roofs covered the entire terrace, held in place by ornate ironwork, only just visible behind the creeping plants that could once have been English ivy, but now seemed to be taking over the whole terrace.

The entire white-painted house looked beautiful, but totally out of place on a tiny Caribbean island.

'The door is open,' said Danielle. 'Let's go find her.'

The entrance hall was just as un-Caribbean as the outside. Larger than it should have been, and serving no purpose other than to remind the owners they had more than enough money, a black-and-white tiled floor was bordered by the ornate plaster walls favoured by the aristocratic gentry of the time. A heavy oak staircase led to the first floor, splitting into two and turning itself into galleried landings that ran around three sides of the space.

'Gee, how the slave traders used to live, huh?' said Aidan.

'We've got plans to get rid of a lot of this opulence, and make it more Caribbean. All in good time though,' said Charlie.

Danielle called out. *'Su Shi... we've brought you some surprise visitors!'*

There was no reply. Danielle called again, but still didn't get a response.

'She must be in the rear garden, clearing some more overgrowth to plant produce.'

She wasn't in the rear garden. Danielle dialled Su Shi's number on the satellite connection. A minute later she killed the call. 'It's ringing but she's not picking up,' she said, a slight tremble in her voice.

'Perhaps she and her phone are not close to each other?' said Daisy, clutching at obvious straws.

'It's possible... we don't call very often, but she's never not answered before.'

They headed back inside the house, calling out as they looked in all the rooms. There was no sign of Su Shi.

'Maybe she's taken a walk? Or gone to see you guys?' said Daisy.

Danielle shook her head. 'There's only one real path, so we would have met her on the way. She might be on the beach though?'

Apart from a couple of giant turtles sunning themselves, the small sandy cove adjoining the lodge was devoid of life too. Daisy narrowed her eyes. 'So where is she?'

Charlie shook his head. 'I have no idea. There really isn't anywhere else that's easy to access.'

'Let's get back to the house.'

Between them they explored the lodge again. Daisy noticed something in Su Shi's bedroom. 'Her bed is turned down ready for sleep and the mosquito nets are closed, but the bedclothes or pillows aren't crumpled. It's like she got ready for bed, but then never slept in it.'

'The kettle is stone cold too,' said Aidan. 'There would have been some residual warmth if it had been used today.'

'And no breakfast pots, either waiting to be washed or on the draining board,' said Danielle.

'Okay Charlie, so where would she have gone?' said Daisy.

He looked frantically around the kitchen, like he was searching for answers that weren't there. 'I can't imagine... most of the area surrounding the compound is still overgrown. Apart from the path to ours and the one to the beach, there isn't anywhere else to go right now...'

'The front door was open.'

'I know. She's likely gone somewhere, but I have no idea where.'

Daisy switched into action. 'Okay, we need a wider search of the area. Split up, everyone.'

They spent the next hour searching everywhere they could. The compound immediately around the house had been cleared of the years of overgrowth, but the wider area surrounding that still needed work. It wasn't too bad, not so difficult to find their way through.

'Mind the snakes, dear,' Daisy called out.

'*What?* Snakes? Have I ever told you I have a snake phobia?'

'Maybe wearing shorts wasn't the best idea then, Dip.'

'Now you tell me.'

They didn't see any snakes. They didn't see a Su Shi either. Eventually Daisy called them together. 'We've got to accept she's not here, guys. Might she have gone for a dip in the sea, and got into trouble?'

The harrowed look on Danielle's face gave away her fear. 'It's possible, I know she takes an occasional swim. But you saw the sea... after the hurricane it's like a millpond, and has been for a full day.'

'No lethal jellyfish or anything?'

'Not that we've ever seen, but...'

Daisy nodded her head. 'Let's go up to her bedroom.'

'Dear?' said Aidan curiously.

In the room, Daisy wrenched open the drawers. There weren't so many filled, Su Shi still collecting clothes after not having arrived on the island with many. 'Does Su Shi skinny dip?'

Danielle shook her head. 'We took a swim together a couple of weeks ago. She wore the black bathing suit I gave her then.'

'This one?' Daisy held it up.

'Um, yeah. It sure looks like it.'

'So unless she's taken a leaf out of Aidan's book and gone au naturelle, she didn't do a Neptune.'

'*Excuse me...*' Aidan protested.

'Bro, you never said.'

Daisy tapped Charlie on the arm. 'Just winding you both up. It's my way of coping with worrying scenarios.'

'It's worrying alright. Where the hell is she?'

'Right now I've no idea. I suggest we get back to the main house, have a nice cup of tea, and decide what to do.'

Just as they walked back through the sitting area, Danielle dialled Su Shi's number on the satellite phone again.

This time it rang for everyone to hear.

Aidan picked it up from the floor, where it had fallen right next to the coffee table, partially hidden from their sight. 'Well, we know where her phone is now.'

Daisy shook her head sadly. 'Indeed. And it has also answered my earlier question. Now we know for sure Su Shi and her phone are not close to each other.'

Chapter 17

'There could be an innocent explanation.'

Daisy threw one of her *stop-trying-to-be-positive* stares at Aidan. He knew what it meant of course. 'What? There could be.'

'You don't really believe that, dear.'

He lowered his head to the lunch table. 'No I don't.'

Daisy addressed them all. 'We have to look at all possibilities, no matter how remote. Su Shi is missing, and I'm sorry to put it so bluntly, but...'

'But she is,' Danielle finished the sentence for her.

'The fact her phone was on the floor almost hidden by the coffee table might be telling.'

Surely you don't think..?' said Charlie.

'Unlikely as it might sound, is there anyone else on Emerald Island, guys?'

Charlie shook his head violently. 'No... no, of course not.'

'Are you sure? Have you explored the whole place?'

'Well, no. It's only six miles long, but the western tip closest to southern Venezuela is covered by impenetrable jungle. There seemed little point in fighting our way in there.'

'How close is the lodge to where the serious jungle starts?'

'Less than a mile, but... are you saying..?'

Danielle pointed something out. 'We cruised around the whole island a few months ago. That end of the island is all but impenetrable, and we didn't see any boats moored anywhere, or signs of life.'

'No inlets or anything?'

'Well there was one we noticed, but it was blocked by fallen trees.'

'What about boats coming and going?'

'We see the occasional one cruise by, but most of the traffic across the Gulf of Paria passes to the north of the island. I can't deny there is plenty of commercial and leisure traffic around though.'

'So someone could have landed on the western end without you knowing.'

Charlie leant his head on shaking hands. 'I suppose it's possible. We just never thought...'

Aidan made a relevant point. 'Flower, if you're thinking that someone chasing Su Shi because of her past has found her, I can't see how they did. She came here in total secrecy, and she's hardly sunning herself on Emerald Island for a photoshoot on the front page of Hello magazine.'

'I know that, Dip. I'm just tossing around options.'

Danielle, who once worked for the CIA, nodded her agreement. 'I gotta say, this is looking like someone else is involved, unlikely as it is.'

Charlie's head was still in his hands. 'Oh boy... and we were so careful.'

'Does she ever take a trip to Trinidad with you guys?'

'No... we all agreed it was too dangerous for her to be seen in public, as it were.'

'And there's no way she got off the island under her own steam?'

'Not unless she made herself a raft from old diesel barrels.'

'She was really content here...' said Danielle, wiping away a tear.

Daisy wrapped an arm around her shoulders. 'Hey, I know you two are close friends. If it helps, I don't think she left of her own accord... if she's left at all.'

The head finally lifted from Charlie's hands. 'What are you saying, Daisy?'

'I'm saying I'm getting one of my gut feelings there's someone else directly involved in this... someone as yet unbeknown to us.'

'Daisy, I can't see...'

Aidan interrupted his brother. 'Charlie, you'd do well to listen to my wife's gut.'

'I am, Bro... well, not literally. That would be weird.'

Daisy chuckled mirthlessly. 'Trust me, Charlie. It's nowhere near as noisy as Aidan's anyway. But after lunch I'd like us to take a closer look at the area surrounding the lodge.'

It had just turned three in the afternoon as the four of them stood in the garden, panning their eyes over the white-walled lodge again. Apart from the fact Danielle had closed the front door, nothing had changed. A surprised and delighted Su Shi didn't come running out to greet them. There were no big happy smiles on faces.

Daisy squinted at the impenetrable jungle in the distance to the west. 'I'd like to examine the space between the lodge and the jungle. There's no point looking at any other side.'

'Dear, you seem to be forming a scenario?' said Aidan curiously.

'Dear, Su Shi's phone was half-hidden on the floor. There's a slight possibility she knocked it innocently and didn't realise, but that's not the Su Shi I know.'

'Are you saying she did it deliberately?'

'Back in the days of my MI6 life, we were taught that if we were kidnapped by force, knocking something into a place it didn't normally belong might give others a clue to what had happened. I rather think Su Shi's Triad training might have taught her something similar.'

Danielle threw her a wide-eyed glance. 'So you *do* think for some reason she was taken?'

'It does seem a likely scenario, dears. And given the lodge's proximity to the jungle, I can see only one place her captors might have come from.'

'Lead the way, Jane.'

'Is that Jane of the Jungle?' Charlie asked.

They spent two hours sweeping the area between the lodge and the start of the jungle, fanning out and keeping their eyes on the ground for anything that might have offered a clue.

There was nothing.

Then, as they reached the start of the impenetrable jungle, Aidan called out. *'Guys, you'd better come and see this.'*

Daisy nodded her head sadly as she reached him, her eyes following his pointing finger. 'I take it you guys didn't make that?'

Charlie and Danielle both shook their heads, in a desolate kind of way.

'Looks like my gut was right then.'

A crude track led into the darkness of the jungle. The hacked-away undergrowth either side of it left no doubt it was hardly a natural occurrence. Someone had made it, and done so for a reason. Charlie rubbed a hand across his mouth. 'Um... why would Su Shi have gone to all that trouble?'

Aidan put a hand on his shoulder. 'Charlie, you don't believe that any more than Daisy does.'

He turned away, and lifted his hands from his sides dejectedly. 'Just covering all the bases, Bro.'

Danielle took his hand. 'Daisy is correct... her gut is right. Someone was here.'

'And for whatever reason they took Su Shi. Sorry, Charlie.'

'I... I don't understand...'

'Neither do I,' said Daisy quietly. 'But the answer lies at the end of wherever that path leads. *Come on...*'

Charlie pulled her back. 'Daisy, we can't go rushing in there, not right now. We don't know what we'll find, and the sun is setting. You really want to play Jane of the Jungle in the dark?'

'It's already darker in there anyway with all the trees, Flower,' Aidan pointed out.

Daisy didn't seem fazed. 'Guys... Su Shi might be somewhere in there, in a less than ideal situation. *We have to...*'

Danielle turned her away. 'Daisy, please listen to us. We know this island a lot better than you, and even we wouldn't go in there when it's about to get dark. I know you're action-girl, but we've gotta be sensible. We need to make the expedition at first light.'

'*Bugger.* I suppose you're right. Now I wish we'd found this earlier.'

'We all do, Flower. But we're not going to help Su Shi if we can't see anything. We'll have to get properly prepared, and be patient until morning.'

'Not my strong suit, Dip.'

'Tell me about it.'

After a fraught evening which Daisy spent mostly pacing up and down, Aidan finally managed to persuade her to join him in bed. As they sat up side by side drinking English tea, he took her hand.

'We'll find her in the morning, dear. But we need a good night's sleep first,' he said gently.

'Will we find her? It's blatantly obvious she's been taken by persons unknown, but it's fifty-fifty whether she's still on Emerald Island or not.'

'I suppose she could have been taken at any point in the last couple of days,' said Aidan.

'Exactly.'

'There's one thing worth pointing out though. We went through the tail of hurricane Madeline, the same one that hit this island just before we had the pleasure of its company.'

'What are you saying?'

'I looked closer at the undergrowth that had been hacked away. A lot of it was loose, not attached to anything.'

'So if it had been done before that ridiculous wind it would have blown away?'

'Almost certainly. At the very least it would have been blown into the sides of the path. It all looked to be lying where it had fallen, which would mean it had been hacked away sometime in the last day.'

'I knew you had a galactic-sized brain for a reason, dear.'

He chuckled. 'I'm sure you would have drawn the same conclusion once you'd had time to look at it properly, Flower.'

Daisy nodded ruefully. 'My bad. I got overwhelmed by the emotion of realising Su Shi had been taken, and didn't keep my mind on the options. It wouldn't have happened twenty years ago.'

'Twenty years ago you weren't out of practice, dear.'

'I'm not sure how to take that.'

'Just accept that brilliant mind and insightful gut are still as sharp as ever, but these days they just take a little longer to kick in.'

'Was that the save of the century, Dip?'

'You decide.'

'Give me a few minutes and I'll let you know.'

Chapter 18

'You brought Uncle Bertie's hunting rifle?'

'Sure I did. The barrel folds, so it fitted into the bag,' said Daisy matter-of-factly, as she snapped the barrel back into place and loaded a few boxes of shells into the pockets of her jacket.

'But how did you know?'

'Dip, we had to be prepared for all eventualities. I would have brought the AK-47 if it wasn't at the bottom of the river Nene.'

'Don't tell me your gut was grumbling even before we left England?'

'No, but old habits die hard.'

'Just don't point that thing at Eric Mildew when we get back.'

'Why not?'

'Um... I can't think of a good reason.'

She handed him a tin of boot polish. 'Then shut up and black half my face.'

'Excuse me?'

'When in Latin America... well, almost.'

'Dear, are you planning on taking on Bolivian bandits?'

'It wouldn't be the first time,' she grinned.

Aidan sighed loudly, making a point, and smeared a couple of wide streaks across her cheeks. Then she grabbed the tin.

'Now let me do you.'

'Oh, come on.'

'Dip, what's the point of one of us being camouflaged if the other isn't?'

'I really wasn't anticipating jungle warfare.'

'Neither was I, but it might come to that.'

'I think you're overreacting.'

'So did Su Shi kidnap herself then?'

'No, but...'

'Dip, I've been to this part of the world before... well, Venezuela, Bolivia and the like anyway. Trust me, hurricanes aren't the biggest killer around here.'

'But we're on a tiny Caribbean island.'

'Yes, and only sixty miles from the Latin-American coastline. It might have escaped your notice, but the side of the island we're about to infiltrate is the closest bit of it to Venezuela.'

'By two miles.'

'Even so, be prepared.'

'So now I'm a boy scout?'

'If it helps. Just don't turn into the Lord of the Flies.'

'Now you're really scaring me.'

Charlie appeared in the bedroom doorway, and tried to stifle a chuckle.

'What?' said Daisy indignantly.

'Um... nothing. I just wasn't expecting to be in the company of Mr. and Mrs. Rambo.'

'We're about to tackle the bad guys, Charlie. In a jungle, not so far from Latin America... which if memory serves, is also full of bad guys.'

'I suppose you have a point.'

'Yes I do. So come here and let me black you up.'

'Me?'

'You want to be riddled with bullets?'

'We don't even know if they have guns.'

'So you want to find out the hard way?'

'Do your worst.'

While Daisy did to Charlie what she'd done to his brother, he told them what Danielle was doing. 'We've pulled up the Google map of the island. It doesn't exactly tell us a lot apart from how many bloody trees there are on the western end of the island, but it might be worth taking a look before we start playing Hawaii 5-O.'

Daisy shook her head. 'This isn't violent American fiction, Charlie. This is real life, and our dear friend has been taken. No one's going to pretend they're Liam Neeson, but we do need to find out how the jungle lies.'

'I know. Sorry for being flippant.'

She tapped him on the shoulder. 'It's okay. We're all sick to our stomachs with worry for Su Shi, so we have to do what we can. *You're done.*'

The three of them filed into the large kitchen area, where the big flat-screen TV that doubled as a PC monitor was hung on the far wall. Danielle sat at a desk next to it, scrolling away with a mouse. She looked up as they entered the room. 'I see you're ready for action, guys.'

Daisy raised her eyebrows. 'No silly chuckles like Charlie then?'

'Hey, I'm ex-CIA remember? If there are bad guys lurking in the jungle, we need to be prepared.'

Daisy grinned. 'See? Someone understands!'

Danielle pointed to the screen. 'There's not a lot to see except friggin' trees, but I've panned in as close as I can.'

Daisy squinted at the screen. 'That end of the island looks like the tip of a parsnip.'

Danielle giggled. 'I suppose it does. The whole area is covered by dense jungle, starts off less than a mile wide, and then peters out to nothing at its tip.'

'Is that an inlet I can see, closer to the tip?'

'Looks like it. It's the one we noticed when we cruised around the island a while back.'

'Big enough to get a small boat inside?'

'Yes, I think so. Hard to tell with all the tree cover.'

'Then that's it. There has to be some kind of boat in there.'

'Or there was,' Aidan pointed out.

'We're not even going there, Dip. My theory is there's some kind of bandit gang hiding out there, and for some unknown reason they decided to branch out and explore the rest of the island... and then discovered Su Shi.'

'Why?' said Charlie. 'Very appropriate analogy, by the way.'

'Yes well, branches could be our friends or our foe. As to why... it's likely they decided to make sure they were the only inhabitants, and came across the lodge.'

Danielle was on Daisy's wavelength straightaway. 'If they're hiding out from something, they wouldn't want anyone knowing they were there.'

Charlie turned away, so the others wouldn't see the fear on his face. 'If that was true, she's likely already dead.'

Aidan wrapped an arm around his brother's shoulder. 'Charlie, all the signs tell us she was taken, for whatever reason. If they were simply going to kill her they would have done it at the lodge, not struggled back through the jungle with her.'

'I suppose.'

Daisy decided she had to get practical, and pointed everyone back to the monitor. 'Look, there's the lodge on the satellite map. The jungle tip of the island looks to be only a mile or so long, and triangular shaped. There's not so much of it.'

'Plenty enough to hide anyone who doesn't want to be found.'

'Ah, but they're not banking on ex-CIA and ex-MI6 agents being on the island.'

Danielle chuckled. 'With one ancient hunting rifle between them?'

'You're lucky I had the foresight to bring that.'

'I suppose it still makes a loud noise.'

'Dear, we're both expert in using what's at our disposal, so shall we get going and recce the area?'

'Lead the way, daughter of Rambo.'

Chapter 19

Coming to a halt at the start of the jungle, Daisy hesitated.

'Daisy?' said Danielle, a little concerned.

'Just taking stock, dear. We don't know what we'll find in there.'

'You want Charlie and me to go in alone?'

'Do I hell. Just taking a deep breath, and running through scenarios.'

'I suggest right now we just find out what the danger is, and then based on what we see, regroup at the house to decide our next move.'

'I agree. If Su Shi is still there though you might have to stop me screaming in like a crazed banshee.'

'Don't worry, I will. One of us is less spur-of-the moment than the other.'

'Oh... which one of us, dear?'

'Do I really have to answer that?'

One by one they filed into the darker confines of the jungle, keeping to the narrow path someone else had kindly made for them. Above their heads, the tops of the trees twined together, forming an effective roof and shelter from the Caribbean sun, but turning their enclosed world to a premature twilight.

Despite the fact the rough pathway had been made by people who had taken their friend, they were grateful for it, the overgrowth either side looking far too scary and impenetrable for comfort.

'I assume there are lots of snakes here?' said Aidan in a small voice.

'It's okay, Bro... most of them are harmless.'

'Um, m... most of them?'

Danielle looked back and grinned. 'I've got the med kit in my backpack.'

'That's not exactly reassuring.'

'Best I've got right now.'

Charlie, at the head of the line, suddenly held up a hand. *'Stop.* I can hear something.'

Daisy caught up with him. *'Hmm...* me too. Voices.'

'I can't see anything for all these damn trees.'

'We need to get closer. Stay vigilant, guys.'

Up ahead, a vague smell hung in the humid air. *'Is that fish?'* Daisy whispered.

'Sure is,' said Danielle. *'Not exactly unusual in these parts.'*

Daisy squinted her eyes tighter again, trying to penetrate the tree line. *'I can see something. It looks a bit lighter ahead.'*

'We must be almost at the inlet.'

They kept a crouching position as they edged still closer. The voices grew louder. So did the sound of guttural, male laughter. Then, it wasn't just what they could hear.

'A boat.'

'Another old fishing boat,' whispered Charlie.

'What the hell? So they're just fishermen taking a sneaky break?

Danielle, slightly further to the right, had a better view. *'Even in the Gulf of No Return, we don't usually see innocent fishermen carrying automatic weapons.'*

Daisy shuffled over to her. *'The gulf of what?'*

'That's what they call the Gulf of Paria these days.'

'Um... why?'

'Because the western part of it can be life-threatening. And from what I can see, it looks like we're in the company of pirates.'

'Seriously? Again?'

Aidan joined them. *'I think these are real pirates, dear. The last ones were just Russian gangsters pretending to be pirates.'*

'Just Russian gangsters? Would someone like to explain that sentence?' whispered Charlie.

'Later, Charlie. Now isn't the time to tell you the story of the Black Pearl.'

'The..? Okay, now I'm intrigued.'

'Let's just say a re-enactment of a long-departed Caribbean pirate era is not half as scary as witnessing a real-life twenty-first century scene. Even if there are similarities.'

Danielle was crawling on her stomach to get a closer look. *'Guys, there's an old building just the other side of that small clearing.'*

On the other side of the inlet, a small area had been stripped of undergrowth. A building made from crude logs and a palm-frond roof stood on the far edge of the tiny open space. They counted six men lounging around, but there could have been more inside the rickety old boat. Most of the pirates they could see were sitting on boxes of something they'd clearly pulled from the boat to make simple seats. They weren't boxes of rum. Daisy narrowed her eyes at them in astonishment.

'They look like boxes of...'

Danielle grinned. *'Yes, Huggies.'*

'Now I've seen everything. Pirates with baby contraband?'

'Don't knock it. They fetch a high price in Venezuela... much higher than they do in Trinidad.'

'But why are they here? The pirates I mean, not the diapers?'

'Dunno. Maybe something went wrong, and they're hiding from the few authorities that exist in this part of the world.'

'Makes sense. They look pretty desperate, despite the fact they're laughing.'

Aidan nodded his agreement. Dressed in grubby clothes, bandanas around their heads, and mostly long-haired and bearded, they sure weren't the kind of people you wanted to come across in a dark jungle. Three of them had Russian-made automatic rifles ready for action by their sides, which just added to the simmering terror. He tried to peer inside the crude hut, but the logs were too close together to see anything. 'You think Su Shi is in there?'

'Stands a good chance,' Danielle whispered. 'If they're hiding from the authorities, she could well have become some sort of bargaining tool.'

'Let's hope so,' said Daisy quietly. 'Sorry, I meant... with the likelihood being she's not already dead.'

'Yes, but if she is a bargaining chip I get the feeling they'll not be here long. As soon as they've arranged the details of a handover in return for their freedom they'll be gone. Which, one way or the other, will be the end for Su Shi.'

Daisy glanced to Danielle, her eyes narrowing into the steely determination Aidan knew all too well. 'Then we need to rescue her, right now.'

'What, without a plan? Even if we did get her out, you think they'd take that lying down? You'd have to kill them all... with a hunting rifle, incidentally.'

'I'll give it my best two shots.'

Aidan took his wife's hand. *'Dear, we need to calm down. We've seen what we needed to. Now I suggest we retreat to the house and make a proper plan.'*

'Bugger it Dip, I hate it when you're so sensible.'

Chapter 20

'So you guys think we're in the company of desperate pirates?'

Danielle dropped the plates containing a hastily-prepared lunch onto the table. 'I'm afraid piracy on the high seas and smuggling is rife around these parts. A few years ago the fishermen of the Venezuelan coast saw their livelihoods decimated, so most of them turned to piracy. Guns, drugs, flour and foodstuffs, that kind of thing.'

'And Huggies.'

Charlie chuckled mirthlessly. 'Basically, whatever they can get their hands on in Trinidad. Venezuela is in a hell of a mess right now, so pretty much everything is in short supply. From what we hear, the coastal town of Güiria is the epicentre for smugglers and pirates.'

'A bit like Port Royal used to be, back in another century.'

'What goes around comes around,' said Danielle.

'It still doesn't explain what a band of ruthless pirates is doing on Emerald Island.'

'Maybe it does. Much of the contraband is picked up from Cedros, on the southern tip of Trinidad. Güiria is on the Venezuelan coast fifty miles north-west of this island, but to get there the pirates would have to pass a few miles off our western tip en route to it.'

'It's not inconceivable their boat got into difficulties, or a seaborne robbery went wrong so they had to hide out here.'

'And then discovered Su Shi all by herself.'

Danielle nodded sadly. 'We have to take it as a small mercy they are here because something unfortunate happened to them.'

'How so?'

'Because if they'd come intent on making the place their base, our Chinese friend would be dead already.'

Aidan shook his head. 'Bluntly put, Danielle... but you're right. Even so, they could now be thinking of making Emerald Island their permanent hideaway, which might explain why they went off exploring. Then they lucked out finding Su Shi and realised she was useful, either for ransom or as a bargaining chip to get them off whatever hook they're on.'

'Desperate people, using desperate measures.'

Danielle put a hand on Daisy's. 'Yes, but as I said, a dead Su Shi would be no use to them.'

'Yes dear, so you keep pointing out.'

'Just trying to keep a positive spin on things.'

Daisy let out a little cry of frustration. 'It's even worse for Su Shi. If they do use her as a bargaining tool and swap their freedom for her life, her identity will almost certainly be revealed. Which means she's as good as dead anyway if we don't get her back.' She threw an ironic glance to Aidan. 'And all we came to do was to see if she could help get us off our own hook, and soak up a few days of Caribbean sunshine. Now we're fighting jungle warfare against ruthless pirates.'

'Maybe when we get her back you can still do what you actually came for,' said Danielle.

'I'm glad you said *when*.'

'So what's the plan?' said Charlie. 'Whatever we do it's got to be soon. Five hours until it's dark.'

Daisy ran her hands through her hair. 'We've got one old hunting rifle between us, which fires two slugs before it has to be reloaded. We can't go for a full frontal assault. That would be suicide.'

'A sneaky op then, to find out for sure if she's been captured, and then get her away without them even knowing until it's too late?' said Danielle.

'That's what I'm thinking.'

'We could try and circle around the outside of the clearing, using the undergrowth until we're next to the hut, and get access that way?'

'Sounds like a plan. The *only* plan, let's be honest.'

'We'd better get gone then,' said Aidan. 'No time to lose.'

Daisy glanced furtively to Danielle, who nodded almost imperceptibly. Daisy put a hand on Aidan's arm. 'Not you, dear. Sorry.'

'What? Now you're saying I'm the one who's too old?'

Danielle smiled sympathetically to him. 'Not at all, Aidan. Charlie isn't going either.'

'What?'

Daisy explained what the men didn't want to hear. 'Look at it with clear vision, guys. Four people having to stay hidden while they sneak up on desperate pirates? Surely you can see the obvious?'

Aidan glanced around the room, looking for divine intervention that wasn't there. 'But... but... then Charlie and me will go...'

'No you won't. Your chivalry is admirable, Dip, but misplaced.'

'Um... why?'

'Because Danielle and I might be retired, but we have vastly more experience than you two of this kind of sneaky operation... and two people are far less likely to be spotted than four anyway.'

'I can't argue with that. But...'

'But nothing. In truth we really only need one person, but quite honestly I don't want to face that dark jungle alone... and I doubt Danielle would either.'

'Got it in one, Daisy.'

'But... but it's dangerous...' Charlie spluttered.

'Then that's all the more reason the two people go who stand a greater chance of success.'

'I... I don't know how to argue that either,' said Aidan, realising that he really didn't.

'Then don't. Just come with us to the edge of the jungle, give me a hug to send me on my way, and wait for three people to come running back out.'

'I definitely can't argue with that.'

'Then let's go, while we've still got some daylight.'

Chapter 21

The four of them stood at the edge of the jungle, and Aidan did what he promised and gave his wife a rather nervous hug.

She smiled a weak smile. 'Chill out, dear. We'll be back before you know it, with Su Shi for company.'

'I wish I knew that for sure.'

Danielle hoisted the scythe over her shoulder she'd grabbed from the tool-shed. 'Keep the faith, guys. We're armed and dangerous.'

Charlie shook his head. 'A garden scythe isn't much of a defence against machine guns.'

She grinned. 'Dork. It's to clear away the undergrowth, which we need to do if we're going to reach the hut without walking brazenly across the clearing.'

'And maybe to chop someone's head off,' Daisy added.

'Dear, that really isn't helping.'

'Just kidding. We'd be gunned down before we got close enough to do that.'

'Dear...'

'Sorry.' She kissed Aidan on the cheek. 'I know waiting patiently isn't your favourite pastime, but try and understand.'

'I am... but are we just supposed to stand here like mannequins?'

'Go back to the lodge if you prefer.'

'We'll stand here like mannequins.'

Aidan and Charlie watched the two women disappear into the gloom of the jungle. They turned away and sat down, and for two minutes tried to do as they were told. Then Charlie threw frustrated hands in the air.

'It's all very well being told to act like crash dummies, Ade, but it seriously goes against the grain.'

'The girls are right though, they are more experienced at this kind of thing than us.'

'And your point is?'

'I... I suppose we might jeopardise the rescue.'

'And what if they get into trouble, get captured too or something?'

'Um... I can't really answer that, can I?'

'No, but I can.'

'Charlie?'

'I'm going to follow them... a kind of rearguard if you like. Not to interfere, but just be there if I'm needed.'

'And what about me?'

'Your call, Bro. Stay here on your own, or come with me.'

'I've got a bad feeling about this.'

'If you come you can stop me doing anything too crazy.'

'That never worked with Daisy, so why should it work with you?'

Charlie grinned. 'I'm not your wife, Ade. We'll hang back and just observe, unless we see or hear anything that requires our intervention. If we're crafty enough no one will know we were ever there.'

'I've still got a bad feeling.'

'So I'm on my own then?'

Aidan let out a huge sigh. 'Lead the way.'

They headed along the narrow path, five minutes behind Daisy and Danielle. One of them kept an eye out to the left, the other to the right. Neither heard nor saw anything.

It was hardly surprising. The density of the undergrowth either side of the crude path meant seeing anything until they were upon it was virtually impossible.

'My snake phobia isn't getting any better,' Aidan whispered.

Charlie looked back to him and shook his head. 'A snake phobia should be the last thing on your mind right now.'

'I thought if I concentrated on my phobia it might take away the other horrors.'

'Keep thinking then.'

They trudged slowly on. Two minutes later Charlie held up a hand. 'I thought I saw something.'

'Are we at the clearing?'

'Not quite. It was a flash of something dark, in the trees over to the right. We should split up a little, just in case.'

'You mean leave the path?'

'Just concentrate on your phobia, Ade. I'll risk the snakes. Let's get thirty feet apart, and then we stand a better chance of spotting whatever it was. If it helps you can stay on the path.'

'It helps. Thanks, Charlie.'

Charlie tapped him on the arm. 'Just keep moving forward slowly. We're close to the clearing, so keep your eyes peeled for any signs of life. Once we're there we'll join up again. No talking for now, okay?'

Aidan swallowed hard. 'I'll say it now then. Good luck.'

Charlie fought his way into the dense undergrowth as quietly as he could. Aidan watched him go for ten seconds, and then began to walk on along the path. A minute later his brother was out of sight, hidden by the trees and the undergrowth.

Instantly, the loneliness hit Aidan hard. He closed his eyes a moment, taking a few seconds to tell himself he'd been in worse situations and come out in one piece. It didn't help much. Daisy had said she didn't much fancy being in the gloom of the jungle on her own, but with Charlie out of sight it sure felt to Aidan like he was exactly that.

Maybe splitting up wasn't the best idea, but Charlie had spotted something, and he wanted them to have the best chance of finding out what it was. He wasn't far away, but he might just as well have been back in Norfolk.

Aidan sucked in a deep breath, forcing himself to remember it was all about being there for his wife, and felt a little better. He opened his eyes again, intending to carry on along the path.

Then he really did hear something. It was impossible not to. Feeling a little better went out of the window in an instant. The click of an automatic rifle chamber was only two feet from his head.

The grinning, bearded face of a pirate in a bandana was just a foot further behind it, and looking like he was itching to pull the trigger.

Chapter 22

They made a slightly strange duo. Two women, traipsing through a dense jungle, both with scarves tied around their heads and cheeks smeared with boot polish, one with a garden scythe over her shoulder, and one with an old double-barrelled hunting rifle at the ready.

The determination on their faces wasn't strange at all though. Their friend had been captured by ruthless bandits, and unless they could do something about it in the next few minutes, it was almost a certainty she would be the subject of an exchange deal.

That meant she was as good as dead anyway. High on the wanted list of several countries for doing things most people actually approved of, she wouldn't last long once her identity was discovered.

They dropped to their knees as the old fishing boat came into view. Three of the bad guys were visible in the small clearing, relaxing as they smoked cigarettes that likely hadn't been bought legally. Danielle pointed sharply to the dense undergrowth to their left.

Daisy nodded. The hut made from logs was on the other side of the small inlet leading off the northern shore, but they could see the end of the water just the other side of the boat. There was a semi-circular route to the hut, but it was completely covered by a mass of jungle vegetation. Somehow they had to use it as cover as they worked their way round to the hut.

Danielle pulled the scythe from her shoulder as they backed away a little. *'Good job I brought this, Daisy.'*

Daisy nodded, and then swallowed hard. *'You know what Aidan was saying about a snake phobia..?'* she whispered back.

'Sorry. It's the only way to get to Su Shi.'

'Tell that to my irrational fears. Just scythe quietly, okay?'

Danielle nodded her head, and began to cut away some of the undergrowth as quietly as she could. One of the pirates was making her job a little easier. He'd rigged up some kind of portable speaker, which was blaring out Latin-American music, in a surreal, echoing kind of way.

The three they could see were tapping their feet as they swigged some kind of alcohol from cans, which also no doubt hadn't been purchased from the local liquor store. They looked relaxed, like they weren't expecting company.

'I wish I knew how many of them there were,' Danielle whispered.

'Me too. Always good to know what the odds are.'

'There's only three visible, but we know there's more, likely lazing in the boat.'

'Let's hope they haven't gone for a walk.'

Progress was slow. Cutting back the undergrowth quietly was a painful, frustrating experience that felt like it took hours. Eventually they were close to the side of the log hut, but still thirty feet from it, and still hidden by the undergrowth.

Together they knelt down, taking a moment to assess the situation.

'Look, that's the door. Su Shi must be inside. It appears to be secured by a single padlock.'

'Why hasn't she just cut her way through the palm-leaf roof?'

'She's likely tied up. And that guy keeping guard isn't helping.'

A fourth guy was standing close to the hut, an automatic rifle in the crook of his tattooed arm. He looked bored to death, but was obviously there to make sure the prisoner didn't escape.

'That's a bugger,' Daisy whispered.

'It sure is. We can't get anywhere near that door without him noticing.'

Daisy pulled out a small pouch from her pocket. 'We need some kind of diversion.'

'What's that you've got?'

'A lock-picking kit, from back in the day. I knew it would come in handy sometime.'

'We still need a diversion. The hut doorway can't be seen from the boat, but that sentry will see us straightaway.'

'Any suggestions, without either of us getting a bullet in the brain?'

As things turned out, they got a diversion without even trying. It just wasn't the kind of distraction they wanted.

A shout from somewhere in the jungle made everyone glance up. The pirates started moving in a concerned kind of way. Three other men appeared on the deck of the boat, quickly running down a short gangplank to join the others in the small clearing.

The guy playing the music switched off the speaker. All six men grabbed their guns, and fixed their eyes on the undergrowth in the jungle where the shout had come from.

'What's going on?' whispered Danielle, as the two women dropped onto their stomachs to watch developments. Then Daisy noticed something.

'I don't know. But look...'

The guy on sentry duty ran to join the others. The hut was unattended. Daisy grabbed Danielle by the collar of her coat. 'Come on... this is our chance...'

They fought their way a little further round the outside of the clearing. People seemed to be shouting in a language neither of them knew, but it didn't matter. They made it just ten feet from the hut, knowing the crude door couldn't be seen directly from the clearing.

It was the perfect opportunity.

Daisy and Danielle struggled to their feet, and were just about to break cover when they discovered they were too late. Two men appeared, their arms linked to a tall man who clearly didn't want to be there.

Daisy gasped. Danielle pulled her back down, out of sight. They watched in horror as one of the pirates unlocked the door, and shoved the captive inside roughly. In the gloom, they still couldn't see the inside. They couldn't be sure if Su Shi was there.

But they knew who has just been captured. Daisy cocked the gun, and began to get to her feet again. Danielle pulled her back down.

'Are you insane?'

'I can't sit by...'

'It's suicide, Daisy. There's nothing we can do right now.'

'Yes there is... I've got two shots.'

'Daisy...'

She shook her head despairingly, and wiped away a tear. 'The stupid, stupid old bugger...'

Danielle pulled her close. 'He and Charlie obviously didn't do as they were told. But where is Charlie?'

'Saved his own skin, by the looks of it,' Daisy spat out.

'Daisy, you know he wouldn't do that.'

She lifted her misty eyes to the roof of the palm trees. 'I'm sorry. I know he wouldn't. But I've got to do something...'

She was almost on her feet again. Danielle wrenched her to the floor, hard. *'Daisy... stop this. Aidan is imprisoned, not facing a firing squad. Screaming in with both barrels blazing is just going to get everyone killed.'*

'You've got a scythe.'

'I said stop it. We need to get back to the lodge and work out what to do, not freak out like Ninja turtles.'

'But... but it's Aidan, stupid bugger or otherwise.'

Danielle held her tight again, partly to stop her doing a Leonardo. They watched as two pirates clicked the padlock into place and headed back to the boat, and saw the sentry return to his post. Then the music started playing again, just to add another sense of foreboding to the horror of normality.

'We could still create some kind of diversion?' Daisy pleaded.

'What, after what just happened? They'll all be on alert now... and where the hell is Charlie anyway?'

Daisy saw the fear in Danielle's eyes. The craziness melted away. At least *she* knew where Aidan was. Anything could have happened to his brother.

'Come on. You're right, we have to get back to the lodge and regroup. You coming?'

Danielle nodded sadly, and followed Daisy as they made their way back to the well-trodden path.

Chapter 23

Celia was rolling some paint onto the walls in the hallway when someone knocked the front door loudly. It made her jump, more than a little. She wrenched it open.

'You startled me.'

The man in the prim suit tipped his bowler hat. 'I do apologise, madam. I simply knocked on the door.'

'Who are you anyway?' asked Celia, not willing to let him know she already suspected who he was.

'I'm Eric Mildew, here to...'

'Sorry, we've already had the damp proofing done.'

He shook his head disdainfully. 'Oh dear... like mother like daughter.'

'I'm sorry?'

'I'm a senior investigative agent for MI6.'

'Really? Did I take an inappropriate picture at the queen's funeral?'

'Oh please. If you did that's an MI5 matter, as you clearly know.'

'Really? And how would I know that?'

'Please don't insult me, Miss Henderson. I am fully aware you are part of your parents' private investigations agency.'

'Then you know more about me than I do of you, Mr. Mildew.'

'Somehow I doubt that. May I come in?'

'No, you may not.'

The obnoxious man coughed in an embarrassed kind of way. 'Very well. Then we shall conduct our private business on the doorstep. I am trying to locate your mother.'

'Really.'

He let out a deep sigh. 'Yes, really. Is she here?'

'Do you see the car?'

'No, I do not. And I did not see it at Fern Cottage either.'

'That's because it and she are not here.'

He threw his piggy eyes to the sky. 'Obviously. So where is she?'

'Cornwall.'

'Cornwall?'

'I'm sorry... do you have a hearing impediment, Mr. Mildew?'

He threw her a slightly pathetic narrow-eyed stare. 'I would advise you to treat me with respect, Miss Henderson.'

'Why?'

'Because I have the full authority of the SIS... and I have a warrant to search the premises.'

'Oh, really.'

'Please stop saying *really*. Try and think of a different word.'

Celia flashed him a cheeky smile, slowly and deliberately. 'Okay then... how about *bullshit*?'

For a second he looked taken aback. It didn't last long. 'Well, really... um, you know what I mean.' He reached into his inside jacket pocket, and pulled out a folded piece of paper. 'Here. Now may I come in?'

Celia unfolded the paper and scanned the official-looking words written there. 'Yes, bullshit is definitely the right word.'

'I'm sorry?'

'This isn't a court warrant. It's just a letter of authorisation from the SIS, saying you are cleared to use whatever means necessary to prove or disprove treasonous acts.'

'Well, it's the same thing.'

'No it isn't. This gives you no right to enter private homes... as you well know.'

Morbid Mildew looked a little flustered, realising he'd attempted to fool the wrong victim. 'Well, um... I can get one.'

Jack appeared at the door, took one look at the slightly red-faced man, and grinned. 'Inspector Mallory... have we been transported through a portal to an episode of *Father Brown*, hun?'

'You'd be forgiven for thinking so, Jack,' said Celia curtly.

Their visitor flushed even redder. 'Well, rea... well, I say. Inspector Mallo... that's an insult.'

Jack nodded. 'True. He didn't wear a bowler hat, even in the nineteen-fifties.'

Celia brought Jack up to speed. 'Mr. Mildew has tried to fool me with a search warrant that's fake, Jack dear. I think you should escort him off the premises... before I do something physical and painful he and I might regret.'

Jack grinned again. 'Hun, I know you're a Jiu-Jitsu black belt, but it might be advisable not to prove it right now.'

'Aw, come on hun.'

He put a hand on her wrist. 'Just try and keep your fists to yourself. I know it's hard...'

Morbid Mildew got the message, and backed slowly away. 'I'll not be intimidated by physical violence,' he exclaimed in a small voice, which actually said the opposite. 'I... I'll be back, with a court warrant... for your mother's place, and yours too.'

'Pathetic threats again, Mr. Mildew?' Celia called as he kept on backing away as far as the drive gate, unwilling to take his piggy eyes off his adversary.

Just before he made his escape, he threw out a smirking kind of smile. 'You'll not be grinning soon, either of you. My investigations are just about complete. Perhaps I should inform you it's not looking good for your mother, either for the treason charge, or an additional one of first degree murder.'

'*Murder?*'

He stopped backing away, realising he'd scored a direct hit. 'Yes, murder. It's come to light that earlier this year your mother committed several illegal acts, including the murder of a fellow double-agent... well, triple agent I suppose. So I suggest you make sure she comes back from Cornwall as a matter of urgency, to face the music. *I'll be back...*'

He turned sharply, and walked very properly behind the tall hedge.

'Hmm, if that was supposed to be an imitation of Arnie, it really did sound like Inspector Mallory doing it,' said Jack.

Celia buried her face in his shoulder. 'It's not funny, Jack. Mum's in serious trouble, and I don't know what to do.'

He held her tight to him. 'I know. There's nothing we *can* do, with her and Aidan out of contact. Do you think Mildew will get a warrant?'

Celia nodded. 'That letter he tried to pass off as a search warrant said he could use all necessary means to do what he had to. When he goes to a judge to get a formal warrant, spouting off about treason and murder, he won't be refused.'

'How long until he's back do you think?'

Celia wiped the gloss from her eyes. 'No more than a couple of days. He's got the knives out, and a finger firmly pointed in mum's direction. He'll want to claim his prize as soon as he can.'

'I wish we knew where she and Aidan were.'

'Me too. Wherever they are, it sure isn't Cornwall.'

He chuckled mirthlessly. 'Think I'd already worked that out. Let's hope wherever they are they get home before Mildew turns up again.'

Celia sniffed loudly, and closed the front door. 'I need to get back to painting walls. Anything to take my mind off this crap.'

'I'll help. Maybe we can take each other's minds off this extinction level event.'

'Sure. Just don't use that phrase again, please.'

'Lips zipped, hun.'

'And anyway... Jiu-Jitsu black belt?'

Jack unzipped his lips, briefly. 'It worked, didn't it?

Chapter 24

'Aidan?'

He picked himself off the dusty floor, and focused on the small voice.

'Su Shi... thank god.'

She looked at him like he'd said the wrong thing. 'I do not think you should thank your god that I am imprisoned in a jungle by pirates, and do not know what is to become of me.'

'Oh hell... I'm sorry. I meant that you... that you're...'

'Still alive?'

He lowered his head. 'Yes. I suppose that's what I meant.'

'Sadly, I do not know for how much longer.'

'Don't say that. I'm here now. And Daisy is too.'

Su Shi shook her head desolately. 'Yes you are here, Aidan. But in case it has escaped your notice you are in captivity too, and also have a locked metal restraint around your ankles. At least I have company now though, I suppose.'

He looked sadly at the forlorn Chinese girl, sitting on a seat made of rough logs. The shoulder-length Chinese-style bob was a far cry from the silky, immaculate hair he'd always known in the past, falling lank and dirty across her tear-stained face. Dressed only in a vest top and little else, the rest of her looked like it could do with a hot shower too.

He looked for signs of bruising or harsh treatment, but could see none. 'Have they... abused you?'

She shook her head. 'I have not been here so long, but apart from being locked in this hut I have not been mistreated.'

'That's surprising.'

'Knowing the kind of bandits that travel in the Gulf of Paria, I am surprised too.'

'There has to be a reason. It might be because of what we think has happened, and what is about to happen.'

Su Shi forced a very weak smile. 'It is good to see you, Aidan... but what are you doing here, of all places?'

'I got captured, remember?' he grinned, trying to lighten a very dark situation.

'You know what I mean. Travelling halfway across the world, obviously without telling Danielle or Charlie you were coming until the last moment, there has to be a good reason.'

He hopped over to the log seat, sat down beside her, and recounted a nutshell version of recent events. Her eyes dropped to the floor. 'I do not think I can help you. I still have some of my diaries, as they are precious to me, but I do not think they contain anything that could exonerate Daisy.'

Aidan's eyes followed Su Shi's to the dirt floor. 'Oh dear. All this may have been for nothing then.'

Su Shi took his hand. 'I would still have been taken, Aidan, but at least you and Daisy were here when it happened. That makes me feel a little better.'

'Sorry, I meant from a hoping you might be able to help point of view. As it turns out, in other ways I'm glad we are here too. I messed up, but I know Daisy and Danielle will be formulating a rescue plan as we speak. We just have to hope it's in time.'

Su Shi lifted her eyes from the floor. 'What exactly do you mean, in time?'

'I haven't told you yet what we think these pirates are up to. The likely scenarios are either that their boat got into trouble and they found this island within range, or they attempted to plunder a vessel which turned bad, so they had to hide out. Forgive me for saying this, but that's likely why you are still alive.'

'You think they are attempting to bargain me for money or freedom?'

'Yes, we do. I don't see any signs of torture, so I assume they don't yet know who you are?'

'No. They came the night after the hurricane passed, and took me by surprise. I have been locked in here ever since, but no one has told me anything.'

'Okay... it's only been a day or so then. We think they are negotiating with whoever is most likely to cough up. Having said that, now I've been useless enough to get myself captured they know there are others on the island, so my thinking is they won't be hanging around too much longer. They'll know people are searching for us, and possibly will have contacted someone in authority.'

'That is not good. It shortens the timescale, and means we may be transported off the island sooner than we might have been.'

'I really have put my foot in it, haven't I?'

Su Shi smiled, and took his hand again. 'You are all very brave to come to my rescue, Aidan. I am grateful I have friends... if not for the fact one of them has been captured.'

'I'll take that as a compliment. I'm now wondering what's happened to Charlie. We'd just separated when they found me. Hopefully he escaped, and Daisy and Danielle too.'

'You were *all* coming to rescue me?'

'Well, kind of. Daisy and Danielle told us mere men to wait at the edge of the jungle while they went to rescue you, but... well, we really couldn't. Like a pair of panicking schoolboys we went after them, and... well, you know the rest.'

She dropped her head onto Aidan's shoulder. 'I think perhaps you were the only one inexperienced enough to get captured, Aidan.'

'Wow... thanks.'

'No, I mean there is only one hut here where they can imprison captives. If the others had been caught they would be in here too. The fact they are not should be an encouraging sign.'

He wrapped an arm around her shoulders. 'You're right, of course. I just wish we knew exactly why these bandits are here.'

Aidan got his wish five minutes later. They heard the padlock click open, and then the crude log door was flung aside. Someone stood there neither of them had seen before.

Someone they sure didn't expect.

Chapter 25

Daisy and Danielle stumbled out of the jungle, to find someone sitting forlornly on the ground with his head in his hands. It didn't please Daisy.

'*You*... what the hell were you thinking?'

He looked up as Danielle dropped down beside him and wrapped her arms around his shoulders. 'At least Charlie is still in one piece, Daisy.'

'And thanks to him, Aidan has been captured. I suppose you saw it happen, and ran away?'

He rubbed a hand across his mouth. 'Daisy... I... I'm so sorry. We heard a noise in the trees and split up to try and see what it was. We didn't...'

'Didn't think. You blundering idiots have ruined everything.'

Danielle glared at Daisy. 'Calm down. They were trying to help. They just... well, they just didn't.'

'And now everything is ten times worse. I suppose it was your idea to follow us, Charlie?'

'Um... yeah, it was kind of.'

Danielle turned the glare to Charlie. 'So was it, or wasn't it?'

'Okay, I was the one who said we should make sure you girls were safe. Aidan agreed though. I didn't exactly have to wrench his arm behind his back.'

Daisy turned away and wiped a tear from her eyes, hoping the others wouldn't see. 'I suppose I can understand that. He never was one for patience.'

'*You're* saying that?'

She turned back to Charlie. 'Okay, so we're both as bad as each other. It doesn't alter the fact you ruined everything.'

'How did we?'

Danielle took up the story. 'We were just about to reach the hut and free Su Shi when they brought Aidan into the camp and shoved him inside. After that... well, they were on alert. We managed to get out.'

Charlie lowered his head. 'I'm sorry. We didn't realise how stupid we were.'

Daisy sat down next to him, rubbing her eyes viciously to try and quell the anger. 'I suppose you weren't to know. Truth is, there was a guard at the door to the hut. It was only Aidan's arrival that made him go and see what was happening, which gave us the opportunity to rescue Su Shi.'

'But you didn't make it?'

'No. We were about to make our move when they appeared with Aidan in tow, and locked him inside too. After that the guard was back, and more on alert than ever.'

'What a mess.'

'That's an understatement. Now they know there are other people on the island, so none of us are safe.'

Charlie struggled to his feet. 'We need to get back to the house, and make some sort of rescue plan.'

'Not the lodge?'

'It's too close to the jungle. If they come looking that's the first place they'll try. I'm hoping they don't know about the main house... yet.'

'Good thinking,' agreed Daisy. 'You guys do realise time is running out? If our theories about why we have visitors are correct, they'll be spooked now. It's a distinct possibility they'll bring their plans forward, and leave under cover of darkness.'

'Tonight,' said Danielle, unnecessarily.

'Which means we've got to formulate a plan, and a distraction to help us carry it out and get Su Shi and Aidan free... and we've got to get back in that jungle before they depart.'

'When it's dark,' said Danielle, making another unnecessary but terrifying point.

'Oh boy,' said Charlie. 'We put off exploring that jungle in the daylight, let alone at night.'

Daisy shook her head, knowing he'd made a scary point. 'So you've now explored it in the day, look upon tonight as the time it gets really spooky.'

'Thanks for pointing out what I already knew, Daisy.'

Back at the house, Charlie made them all coffees while Danielle fixed a little food. 'Ideas, guys?'

Daisy looked like all sentient thought had deserted her. 'I'm kind of out of those. We know where they're being held, but I can't think of anything except somehow disarming that guard and picking the lock.'

Danielle glanced to the clock. 'It's three in the afternoon. We've not got long before it gets dark.'

'Yes, but the darkness is both our friend and our enemy.'

Charlie knew instantly what Daisy meant. 'If we wait too long they might be gone, using the darkness to slip away without anyone spotting them. But given the situation, the only way we're going to succeed in a rescue is by also using the night as cover.'

'Don't remind me.'

A knock on the kitchen door made them all jump, until it dawned on them ruthless pirates would hardly wait outside to be let in. 'Come in,' said Danielle shakily.

Willy walked in with a big grin, until he saw the expressions on the faces of the three people sitting at the kitchen table. 'Oh boy. I was going to ask how you all were, but it doesn't look like I need to.'

'No, you don't. We're feeling exactly what it says on the can.'

'No Aidan?'

Danielle indicated for him to sit with them at the table, and then brought him up to speed with the current situation. He listened intently, and then grinned.

'So what you need tonight is a big distraction?'

'Don't look so pleased about it. The rest of us are terrified.'

'Sorry. It's just the ex-president whose character I inherited was expert at distractions... and conflict, come to that.'

'So why are you looking so pleased with yourself?'

'Because I might just have the perfect distraction you need.'

'Please tell us, because we're running out of ideas,' said Daisy, wondering why she was getting excited about what an artificially-intelligent ex-scarecrow had to say.

'Well, I came to see if you guys would like to attend the honours ceremony.'

Charlie threw a frustrated hand into the air. 'Willy, don't you think that's the least of our concerns right now, watching a load of monkeys receiving certificates of excellence?'

'Sure I do. But that's kind of the point.'

'It is?'

He shook his head, like a mechanical teacher losing patience with slow pupils. 'Don't you see? My monkey school has fifty pupils, and we hold intelligent conversations between us all. I'm their head teacher, to coin a phrase, so they listen to me.'

Daisy found her head shaking again, all by itself. 'So I've stumbled in on a remake of *Planet of the Apes*. What has any of this got to do with rescuing our friends?'

'My pupils have at least the same number... the *same* number again of their friends who don't attend the school.'

'Willy, you're still not making sense. Please get to the point.'

'You need a distraction tonight, am I right?'

'Yes, but...'

'Okay, this will make your head spin, but just believe I've not gone as insane as the personality I'm trying to shake off would suggest. I can organise a big distraction, trust me.'

'You can? How?'

'A hundred monkeys!'

Chapter 26

Aidan groaned to himself as the woman in knee-length boots strode up to him. He was getting instant flashbacks of the one previous time he'd been kidnapped by a beautiful woman in boots, and it wasn't boding well for his future.

This one looked a lot more menacing than Irina the Russian KGB agent, who he'd eventually become friends with, and who possessed the softer side he'd managed to unearth before she died.

This one looked like she didn't even know what a soft side was.

'Cómo se llama?' she spat out as she stood with her long legs apart, glaring down at him.

He looked her up and down. She was black... all black, except for the flawless tanned Latin-American complexion. Clad in a skin-tight black one-piece leather suit and black boots, a shock of long, intentionally-untamed curly black hair completed the menacing blackness.

'Sorry, I don't speak Spanish,' he said, even though he knew exactly what she'd said.

Her bright red lips curled into a smile that was just as threatening as the rest of her. 'Ah, so you are English man.' She leant down, so her beautiful face was inches away from his. 'I said, *what is your name?*'

'Um... Fred. What's yours?'

She stretched back up, and placed her hands defiantly on her slim hips, making sure he knew who was in command. 'Ha! You have balls, Englishman, I will give you that. Imprisoned in a jungle by people who will kill you as soon as look at you, yet you demand to know my name?'

'I just thought it would be nice to know who will end my life in a few minutes time.'

She shook her head, animating the rampant curls into a mesmerising blur. 'You think I wish to kill you? Do you see a big gun in my hands?'

'Um... no, but those two thugs in the doorway appear to be packing Russian automatic rifles.'

'*Thugs?* You insult my trusted men? Perhaps I will kill you after all.'

It was Aidan's turn to shake his head. 'Please don't. I apologise profusely.' Then he took a punt, realising there was little left to lose. 'If my guess is right, my... um, girlfriend and I are worth more to you alive.'

'*Girlfriend?*' She glanced in disbelief to Su Shi, who had her head bowed. 'If she did not look Chinese I would say she was your daughter, not your girlfriend.'

Aidan glanced to Su Shi, hoping she would clock onto where he was going with his lies. 'So there's a bit of an age gap. We love each other.'

The woman in black strode over to the much younger Su Shi. 'Is this true? You are partner to this old man?'

'Excuse me?' said Aidan, trying to sound indignant.

Su Shi looked up, and fixed dull eyes into the woman. 'Yes, we are together.'

'*Arrgh...* that is so disgusting. No matter.' She stomped back to Aidan. 'I do not care what you get up to, but I do care how many other people are on this island. So tell me, old man.'

'I'll tell you, if you give me your name.'

A hand whipped out and slapped Aidan hard across the face, reminding him of Irina when she'd first kidnapped him. *You try to bargain with me, when you are in no position to do so?'*

He shook his head, and then rubbed his smarting cheek. 'That's the deal, whoever you are.'

She turned away, realising her captive really did have balls, and the only way to get information out of him was to give a little back.

'My name is Carla. That is all you are getting.'

'So what are you doing on my island, Carla?'

'*Your island?* You own this inhospitable clump of trees?'

'Yes. Lucy and me live here... alone.'

'Ah. So there are no more English peoples? Or Chinese?'

'Just us. I came to rescue Lucy.'

Carla laughed. Even her mirth sounded menacing. 'Forgive me, my friend, but you did not do a very good job.'

'So I'm just a senile old man, remember?'

'Sure I do. And now I have two hostages.'

Aidan nodded, making sure Carla saw. 'So you do intend using us as bargaining chips for your freedom. Wanted by the authorities then, Carla?'

She stormed back to glare lightning into his eyes, reminding him of the hurricane he experienced a couple of days previously. *'That is not your concern,'* she spat out.

'I think it is. You trespass on my island, take my girlfriend prisoner while I was out hunting, and then capture me. Now you hold us both captive, and we do not know what will become of us. Do you not think the least we deserve is an explanation?'

She lifted an arm to slap him again, but then thought better of it and turned away, letting out a Spanish expletive or two. 'Very well, as you are nothing but a nosy Englishman. It will do no harm to tell you now. Our current situation is not exactly a secret from the police anyway.'

'So go on then... I'm listening... and I'm not going anywhere.'

She strode over to the other side of the small hut. 'Not for a few hours you are not. We are waiting to hear from the police in Caracas. As soon as they agree to our terms we will be sailing to Güiria to exchange you for our pardon.' She gave him a sweet smile. 'Except now we have twice as much bargaining power, with a rich Englishman who will lose his life if we do not get what we want.'

'So you *are* a wanted woman then?'

Carla sighed, a force of hot air that seemed to shake the log walls of the hut. 'It became too dangerous is Caracas. This last year the man I love was killed by the police, when they drafted many officers into the town to flush us out.'

'It obviously worked.'

Aidan got another glare of green fire. 'I made a considered decision, understand? I was captured but managed to escape. They have been looking for me ever since. We decided the mainland was too risky, so now we live in the Gulf of Paria, and... do business here.'

'We?'

'I joined forces with a few of Carlos's loyal men who were not killed. Now we survive mostly on the water.'

'In an old fishing boat?'

That made the delayed slap finally land. 'It is temporary. And our boat may be old but it is full of new technology, which will assist us to obtain our pardon.'

'I see,' said Aidan, rubbing his face again. 'And please stop slapping me. It's getting annoying now.'

'You want me to shoot you instead?'

'Oh, and murder one of your bargaining chips?'

Carla turned away, clenching her fists together. 'I offered to exchange you for my freedom alive, not undamaged.'

'Is that a threat?

She glanced back to her captives, but seemed unwilling to answer. 'I am leaving you now. There are preparations to make. Do not even think about escape. There are now two guards on the door, so even if you did manage to evade them you will not get far with those electronic restraints around your ankles.'

Aidan glanced down to the secure shackles. 'Part of the new technology you people are using now, hey?'

'Sure.'

She waved to the two thugs to leave the hut. Just as she reached the doorway, Aidan called out. 'Excuse me, Carla dear... how much longer do we have to stay in this hut? I have a snake phobia.'

She animated the curls, and laughed again. 'You English, so wimpy. Do not fear, Fred... once it is dark we are out of here, so you will not have too much longer to die from a snake bite.'

Once they were alone, Su Shi threw Aidan a weak smile. 'I was not aware we were having an affair, darling.'

He grinned back. 'I thought if I pretended we were in a relationship it would add more credence to the fact we were living on the island alone.'

'Yes. It would not be good if they knew there were others here.'

Aidan nodded slowly. 'Indeed. Others who will undoubtedly attempt a rescue.'

'You do not sound entirely happy about that.'

'Let's just say there isn't long for them to do it. Carla let slip we would be leaving the island once darkness fell, and knowing Daisy she won't risk anything without the cover of the night either.'

'You are thinking they might be too late?'

He closed his eyes to ward off the images he had no chance of not imagining. 'It's a possibility. But I also know my wife will do anything to rescue us. I'm just silently begging her not to attempt something too crazy.'

Chapter 27

'A monkey battalion?'

Willy grinned as only he could. 'Sure. They'll do their stuff if I ask them nicely.'

'Seriously? You do remember who your character is based on?'

'I told you I'm trying to shake his influence off. I still get the urge to mediate between the warring factions occasionally though.'

'And I didn't think things could get any weirder.'

Charlie laughed. 'Actually Daisy, monkeys are way more intelligent than humans give them credit for.'

'Exactly,' said Willy. 'And as I'm not human I'm the perfect one to make it happen.'

'So what... you going to arm them with AK-47's and hope they don't hit one of us?'

'Now you're delving into the realms of fantasy.'

'Um...'

Danielle interceded before Daisy blew a fuse. 'I think what Willy is proposing is that a hundred or so screeching monkeys would create sufficient chaos for us to slip in and rescue Su Shi and Aidan.'

'I suppose.'

'You got a better idea?' said an insulted Willy.

'For once, no. The one thing we need is a diversion, so I guess a pack of screaming monkeys will have to do.'

'It's called a tribe.'

'I stand corrected.'

Charlie narrowed his eyes at his creation. 'Willy, are you sure you can pull this off? I know you've been teaching them, but...'

'Don't worry, my maker. Just be prepared to hand out big bananas to those who go above and beyond.'

'Going above and beyond is what worries me,' said Daisy.

'I think you need to meet my tribe,' said Willy.

'So you want me to be Roddy McDowell now?'

'If it helps... but my guys are monkeys, not apes.'

'Hmm... even now you have an answer for everything.'

'Does that make your head spin? Oh, sorry.'

Charlie stood up from the table, before the present became too much like the past. 'How long do you need to assemble the troops, Willy?

He thought a moment. 'I need to round up the pupils and bring them up to speed, then they need to pass on the word to their friends to make up the numbers... a couple of hours?'

'That's about as much time as you've got. It'll be getting dark by then. Assemble everyone on the front lawn as soon as you can, okay?'

Willy saluted, and disappeared to rally the troops. Daisy shook her head. 'This is just insane enough for Maisie to believe it.'

'Who?'

'Never mind, long story. I'm going to go polish the hunting rifle.'

A half-hour later Danielle sat down beside Daisy, who still had an air of disbelief about her. 'I know you think we're all insane, but I've seen how Willy teaches the monkeys, and how they respond to him. I realise it's difficult for someone from outside the island to get her head around the strange and mysterious, but... well, do we have a choice?'

'I've seen a lot of strange and mysterious in my life, Danielle, but apart from Willy himself this takes the biscuit. Well, banana maybe.'

Danielle giggled. 'At least you can still be witty.'

'It's about all I have left.'

Danielle pulled Daisy into her, and brushed away the mistiness from her eyes. 'Have a little faith. We'll get Aidan back, and Su Shi too.'

'We still don't know if either of them are still alive.'

'I think we do. The theory about Su Shi, and now Aidan, as bargaining chips is a sound one.'

'Yes, it is. But it could still be wrong.'

'I can't deny that. For what it's worth though, I think it's on the money. And I know these parts a lot better than you. Corruption and deals with criminal gangs are pretty much the norm here. In large parts of Venezuela gangsters are hero-worshipped.'

'So you're saying if Aidan and Su Shi are being used to barter freedom there's a chance they'll succeed?' said Daisy.

'Yes. And the bandits know it. Aidan and Su Shi are worth far more to them alive.'

'I guess they lucked out with them both then?'

'It's almost a certainty, in my mind. And from what we saw, it looks like they're both in the same log cabin.'

'We just have to hope we and the monkeys get there before they're gone, because I get the feeling tonight's the night in more ways than one.'

Danielle stood up to leave. 'And it's going to be a hell of a showdown. I know it's unlikely to happen, but try and get a little rest before we leave... deal?'

'I'll try. No promises.'

Daisy closed her eyes for a while, knowing sleep would be impossible. Fear for Aidan and Su Shi ran riot inside her mind, and made for a very effective poke in the ribs each time she felt herself drifting away.

Their theory *was* pretty sound, but that just added to the terror building up inside her. Now that the pirates had doubled their hostage take, it was even more likely they'd be on the move as soon as they could.

Aidan wouldn't let on there was anyone else on the island, but the chances were the pirates would not totally believe him. There was a strong possibility they would believe those not in captivity would raise the alarm to the authorities, and the island they thought would make a nice uninhabited home would before very long be crawling with the exact people they were hiding from.

Whichever way she came at it, time was rapidly running out.

Daisy might not have believed sleep would come, but exhaustion said otherwise. A gentle hand on her shoulder brought her back to reality. Danielle smiled down to her.

'It's time, Daisy. Get yourself together.'

Almost cursing herself for drifting off, as the fog cleared from her brain it did so from her ears too. 'What's that noise?' she mumbled, still half-asleep.

Danielle, standing at the door to the first-floor balcony, beckoned to her. 'Come and see.'

Daisy went and saw, and then cried out in disbelief. The lawn wasn't so big, but it wasn't that small either. She could see hardly any of it. *'You have got to be kidding me...'* she whispered in an awe-inspired kind of way.

In the gloom of the setting sun, the lawn was covered with monkeys. The air was filled with monkey-chatter, which got louder as Willy's assembled battalion spotted the two women standing on the balcony. Willy himself was marching up and down, barking out a rallying pep talk to his hairy privates. Then he realised what his troops had seen, and turned to grin to the balcony. He saluted, as all generals do.

'All present and correct, commander,' he called out.

'I think I'm still dreaming,' said Daisy, still trying to shake some sense into her head.

Danielle giggled. 'It's real, Daisy. So wave to your distraction detail.'

Daisy half-lifted a hand, and quietly moved it from side to side in a regal kind of way, wondering what she was getting herself into. The chattering grew deafening, the troops clearly appreciating the fact their commander had acknowledged they were a force to be reckoned with.

Daisy nodded slowly, and turned back to the room. 'How can I ever look at a banana in the same way ever again?' she mumbled.

Danielle grabbed her hand. 'I told you Willy would do his stuff. Now all you've got to do is accept the unacceptable and lead your troops into battle.'

'That might be easier said than done.'

'Just think of them as hairy human privates, ready and willing to obey your every command.'

'Or every banana?'

Danielle chuckled, clearly amused by her friend's disbelief. 'Just visualise whatever it takes to make it happen.'

They headed downstairs. A blacked-up Charlie was waiting for them in the kitchen. He handed them both a brandy. 'Thought you might need this, Daisy,' he said, a smile on his face.

'You're loving this, aren't you? Am I only allowed one drink?'

'No time to lose, and we need you sober anyway.'

'I was starting to think I'd accidentally eaten some magic mushrooms.'

'Welcome to Emerald Island.'

Daisy downed the brandy in one swig. 'If I said heading into jungle warfare with a monkey battalion was one thing I didn't anticipate doing, would you believe me?'

'Actually I would, yes.'

'Then you know how I'm feeling right now.'

Charlie took her slightly-shaky hand. 'Sure you're up for this?'

'Bizarre as it is, it's for Aidan and Su Shi. What do you think?'

Charlie nodded his answer, and grabbed a couple of powerful torches. 'Then get your gun, Annie, and lets go kick ass.'

'Let's hope there's still ass there to be kicked, hey?'

Danielle fastened her scarf back around her head. 'It's not quite dark yet. Those pirates will still be there, with no idea of what's about to hit them.'

Daisy shook her head for the hundredth time that day. 'They're not the only ones.'

Chapter 28

'I can hear something, Aidan.'

Su Shi hopped over to the wall nearest to the clearing, and tried to squint through the tiny gaps in the logs. 'I cannot see much, but it looks like they have rigged up some kind of light in the clearing.'

Aidan heard the muffled sound too, and tried to reassure his friend. 'They're running the boat engines to charge up the batteries, that's all. If they've rigged up lights they won't want them draining the power.'

Su Shi turned to look at him, and even in the darkness he could see her eyes were full of fear. 'Or on the other hand they are preparing to leave.'

'Well, I suppose that's a possibility too.'

Then they heard something else. The padlock was being unfastened. They both hopped quickly to the crude log bench and sat down. The door swung open, and the grinning face of one of the pirates walked in, two metal plates in his hands.

'Hey gringos... I bring you food.'

Aidan looked at the plate he was handed. 'Um... what is it?'

'It goat stew. It good. You eat, yes?'

'That's... very kind of you.'

'Sure it is. We don' want the police thinking we don' treat our hostages right, see?'

'Other than imprisoning them in a hut made of logs, yeah?'

'Sure. But not for much longer, Englishman.'

'What do you mean?'

The obnoxious grin didn't fade. 'You eat quickly, yes? Soon we go to Güiria to hand you over in exchange for our freedom. It all sorted now.'

'All sorted?'

'For sure. Carla say to thank you for your cooperation.'

'Like we had any choice,' said Aidan ruefully.

The pirate headed to the door. 'Eat, gringos. In an hour we go from this place, and you tell the police we treat you good, yes?'

'Oh yes, we will,' said Aidan subserviently.

Su Shi took a mouthful of the stew. 'You should eat, Aidan. It is not so bad, if you have sharp teeth.'

'It's not easy to eat, when we're about to go get handed over to people who will soon realise who you are, Su Shi.'

'It does not matter about me. I always knew one day I would need to face judgment for what I have done.'

'It matters to me. All you did was eliminate people that most of the planet agreed deserved it. And where the hell is Daisy anyway?'

'It is only just dark, Aidan. Outside this jungle there will still be light in the sky. I am sure they are on their way.'

'And now the bad guys have rigged up lights, so they'll see them coming.'

Su Shi wrapped her hand around his. 'Keep the faith. Both Daisy and Danielle know what they are doing. Their past careers, remember?'

'I still have a bad feeling. I wish those boat engines weren't running.'

She nodded. 'It is not a good sign, I know. But let us look on the positive. If Carla and her henchmen leave this island, with or without us, then at least they will be gone and life can return to normal.'

He gazed at her with sad eyes. 'It won't be normal for you, Su Shi. Incarcerated in a Venezuelan prison is most people's idea of hell.'

'Perhaps it will not come to that. They may not realise who I am.'

'You really believe that?'

Su Shi picked up Aidan's fork, and shoved a chunk of goat's meat into his mouth. 'Eat, my friend. When the others get here you will need every bit of your strength.'

Aidan chewed the tough meat. 'You didn't answer my question.'

She lowered her head, and spoke quietly and deliberately. 'I have told you, my destiny is unimportant. I achieved my lifelong goal, which is the one thing that mattered to me. Now there is something else that matters... that my good friends go on to enjoy their lives, even if I am not there to see them do so.'

'Now I feel like I need to cry.'

Chapter 29

They made a bizarre sight. Three humans, their faces smeared with boot polish war paint, one artificially-intelligent ex-scarecrow, and a battalion of a hundred monkeys hurrying across the scrub between the lodge and the start of the jungle would be a sight to behold in any part of the world.

Daisy shook her head yet again as she followed Danielle closely. Even Steven Spielberg would have difficulty imagining the strange and wondrous scene.

She was still considering the fact she might wake up at any moment.

Willy raised a hand as they reached the start of the jungle. 'Silent running now, guys.'

'That's for submarines,' said Daisy.

'Okay, you know what I mean. The element of surprise is crucial.'

'You're telling me that?'

He held a finger to his lips, indicating to his men to cease chattering, and to work their way slowly into the trees. Somehow the well-drilled troupe seemed to understand him. In seconds they were disappearing into the dark jungle, not a chatter amongst them.

Danielle dragged a bemused Daisy with her along the hacked-away path. 'Come on, Daisy. Yes, you are awake. Time to be the Daisy we all know.'

Charlie grinned as he took position at the rear of the line. 'Just pretend it's a movie scene.'

'It is a movie scene. With real bullets.'

They worked their way closer to the small inlet, their monkey allies swinging through the trees silently just above their heads. Then Willy stopped, and held up a hand. His advanced hearing had caught a sound. *'I can hear boat engines, guys,'* he whispered.

'Oh no,' said Charlie.

'I can't hear anything. You sure you haven't got a twisted cog or something?' said Daisy.

Willy was just about to retort indignantly, but Charlie did it for him. *'I gave him acute hearing. He'll hear things before any human.'*

'I'll take your word for it, wizard. Let's get closer.'

Five minutes later their world got a little lighter. As the three of them dropped to their knees it was clear why. A twin lamp on a tripod stand illuminated the clearing, together with the exhaust water spitting from the outlets at the stern of the old boat.

'They're leaving...' said Daisy in a dismayed kind of way.

Danielle tried to smile reassuringly. *'Well the engines are running, for sure. But they haven't left yet, and we're here now. They're charging the batteries before they go, especially with that powerful light to power.'*

Charlie nodded his agreement. *'They're taking no chances. They know if they stay in the dark they're vulnerable to possible attack.'*

Daisy clicked the barrel of the hunting rifle into place. *'They're vulnerable alright. Let's go, before they do.'*

Charlie and Danielle pulled her back down. *'Are you insane? We need a game plan. Blundering in there with a double-barrelled shotgun is a sure-fire way of saying goodbye... to everything.'*

Daisy tried to glare them both into submission, but then gave in and accepted they were right. *'But they've got Aidan...'* she whispered in a small voice.

Willy dropped down beside them. *'And we'll get him and Su Shi back. We'll get them back... oh sorry, repeating myself again.'*

'Just don't spend an hour and a half spouting off a rallying speech, okay?'

'Those days are over, trust me.'

Danielle grinned despite the gravity of the situation, and then brought them all back to the present. *'Okay... Willy, your task is to take command of the distraction. We still don't know how many of them there are. I can see three in the clearing, enjoying what is no doubt a last ill-gotten beer on solid ground, but I guarantee there are more in the boat.'*

'And without question they've all got guns, se we can't just go screaming in. We'll get shot before we get ten feet, most likely out of their sheer surprise.'

'So what do we do then?' said Daisy.

'Let our monkey battalion confuse the hell out of them first, and when they don't know whether they're in a Disney movie or not, we'll sneak into the hut and rescue the guys.'

'We need to work our way around closer to it then, like Danielle and me did before Aidan ruined everything.'

'Bluntly put, but yes.'

Willy nodded. *'I'll instruct the guys to use the trees to encircle them, and then when I give the word all hell will break loose from every direction. They won't know what's hitting them. You could say it'll make their heads spin.'*

'Well, you could.'

He grinned. *'Old habits die hard, huh? We all agreed?'*

The three humans nodded, one of them not quite as enthusiastically as the others. Willy crawled away, and then they saw him talking to one of the bigger monkeys, who had procured an army sergeant's cap from somewhere. He listened intently to his commander's words, and then ran off. Willy shuffled back. *'Three minutes. The troupe is making its way through the trees to circle the enemy camp. As soon as they're in position I'll give the signal, and then the fun starts.'*

'Fun? I never did like monkeys, ever since one of them pinched my ice-cream at London zoo when I was a child.'

'Hmm... ice-cream. You got plenty in stock for when this is over, guys?'

'Somebody poke me in the ribs and wake me up before it's too late.'

Chapter 30

Alfredo took a swig of his ill-gotten beer, and then spotted something. He grinned to Eduardo. 'Hey padre, that monkey there in the trees looks hungry.'

Eduardo followed his eyes. 'He's got a mate too.' He called out to his two visitors. 'Hey Chico, you want some goat stew? Oh sorry, it all gone.'

The three men laughed, and took collective swigs of the beer. Then Alfredo saw something else. The grin faded slightly. 'Compadre, they is more of them now.'

The three men glanced around the trees bordering their little clearing. Eduardo shook his head. 'It a family. A big family.'

'Yeah, sure. Guess they is wanting food.'

'Do monkeys eat goats?'

'How should I know? They all got their beady eyes on us.'

'Maybe they eat humans too.'

Alfredo swallowed hard. 'Nah. They's just monkeys. What harm can they do?'

'They don' seem to be sayin' much. Just starin'.'

The three men swivelled their heads. Monkeys seemed to be everywhere, the light from the powerful lamp glinting off their dark unblinking eyes.

'Why ain't they doing something? Don' monkeys swing from trees or make stupid noises?'

'They don' do that all the time. Sometimes they gotta rest.'

'They's resting now for sure. Just starin', like they knows something. Giving me the creeps, compadres.'

Eduardo threw his metal plate at one of their visitors. It missed, but the monkey didn't flinch. He looked wide-eyed at his friends. 'He didn't run away. Now I is really spooked.'

About to tell his friend he was just a coward, somehow the words seemed hesitant to leave Alfredo's lips. It might have been something to do with the fact more and more monkeys were joining the throng, and staring at them silently. 'Geez, that is one big family...'

'Maybe we get back to the boat? It almost time to leave anyway.'

The suggestion seemed to meet with approval. The three men stood up warily. It was all they had time to do. Someone hidden in the trees screamed out a whooping war cry.

As the pirates reached for their guns, they knew it was too late.

All hell let loose.

The jungle burst into deafening sound. As the three pirates covered their ears, they realised the incessant screeching was far from the only thing they had to deal with. It seemed like a million monkeys launched themselves from the darkness of the trees. It wasn't quite a million, more like a hundred, but it sure felt like it.

In seconds the scratching, biting animals were all over their prey. Pirate arms flailed around helplessly, a desperate attempt to defend themselves from a crazed attack they never expected. Their human screams mingled with the screeches of the determined aggressors, as more and more of the creatures leapt out of the trees to do battle.

The two guards staggered into view, covered in fighting, gnawing monkeys. The guns in their flailing hands were snatched away, just before they fell to the ground, covering their heads in a desperate attempt to escape serious injury.

Willy, sensing victory, ran into the clearing before the others could stop him, gesticulating at his troupe to finish the job. It didn't occur to him there were more pirates sheltering on the boat.

Three pirates ran onto the deck of the old fishing boat to help their comrades, only to be met with the grinning toothy smiles that weren't smiles at all, inches away from their faces. One of them managed to raise his gun and fire off a few random rounds before he too was overwhelmed.

One of the slugs ripped through Willy's arm, and right out the other side. He looked at it in dismay, and then the grin was back.

'Good job I don't feel pain,' he said loudly.

Fighting off an aggressive monkey, Alfredo, standing six feet away, looked at him in disbelief. *'What?'*

Willy lifted his sleeve. 'I do leak hydraulic fluid though. Look what your pal has done!'

Alfredo looked wide-eyed at the yellow liquid running down Willy's arm. *'Wh... what?'*

Realising he'd given his foe the jitters, Willy twisted the knife. 'Oh, didn't you realise? I'm a robot... *look!*' He twisted round, lifted his tunic, and opened his battery compartment flap. 'See?'

Alfredo shook his head manically, his mouth hanging open with sheer fright. *'Oh mama...* an attack of kamikaze monkeys, and now a mechanical man... who *talks*? *No, no, no...* this it is too much...'

Someone else seemed to think so too. From inside the boat, a woman's frantic voice screamed out. *'Cut the ropes!'*

Carla's panicking face appeared in the wheelhouse, a hand desperately wrenching the throttles into reverse. As the deck became swamped with monkeys, Alberto and Eduardo, through sheer desperation, fought them away, drew knives, and slashed the ropes.

The two who had been on guard, still clad in crazed monkeys, threw themselves at the deck as the engine note rose, and the boat began to reverse out of the small inlet. Then another sound filled the air.

Automatic gunfire echoed around the small clearing. The monkey battalion's sergeant, still wearing his cap, had acquired himself an abandoned automatic rifle, and was firing at the boat as it began to disappear between the trees.

Daisy, running towards the hut with Danielle, screamed at Willy. *'Tell that monkey to stop firing!'*

Willy looked devastated. 'What? They're getting away...'

'Let them go,' shouted Danielle. 'We'll make sure they get apprehended at sea.'

Willy didn't seem to like that. *'No*... we need to capture them...'

The monkey sergeant was still firing slugs into the receding boat. *'Will you tell him to stop firing, for god's sake?* We've achieved our objective. It's all too much noise.'

Willy waved a reluctant hand to his battalion. The gunfire stopped. The incessant chattering stopped. The boat was almost out of sight as the monkeys on the deck leapt off onto dry land, obeying their commander-in-chief.

The jungle fell almost silent. Apart from the scream of the fishing boat's engines as it headed backwards to the open sea, all was still. But then, as Willy's monkey battalion regrouped in the small clearing, a thunderous noise filled the air once again.

Alfredo, realising he was suddenly monkey-free, and still reeling from the embarrassing fact he'd been outwitted by a robot, was determined to seek his revenge. Just before the boat disappeared from view he ran onto the bows, machine gun in hand.

A hail of lightning bolts flashed out in the darkness. There was only one place the slugs were heading. Two of them found their target, slamming into Willy's chest. Standing in the clearing, right next to the water's edge, he cried out and staggered, lost his balance, and toppled into the water.

Daisy lifted her rifle and let off both barrels, but she was too late. The boat had disappeared around a slight bend, and they all knew reaching it in time through an overgrown jungle was never going to happen.

It wasn't the most important thing right then.

Someone was seriously wounded.

Chapter 31

As Charlie waded into the water to reach Willy, Daisy and Danielle ripped off the padlock keeping the hut door secure, and grabbed Aidan and Su Shi as they fell out to meet them.

'What the hell?' Aidan exclaimed. 'There are monkeys everywhere!'

'They were our distraction, thanks to Willy.'

As if to confirm it, one of their hairy friends appeared, and held out a set of keys he'd clearly taken from one of the unfortunate guards. Then, with a dejected-sounding cry, he ran off to see how his commander and head teacher was.

Su Shi looked just as bemused and vacant as Aidan did, but she managed to mumble, *'Willy?'*

Daisy and Danielle undid the electronic shackles, and then Daisy looked at them with sad eyes. 'Yes, Willy. If it hadn't been for his crazy scheme this wouldn't have ended so well. Except it hasn't ended so well for Willy.'

'He's not...'

'I don't know... we need to go see...'

The four of them ran to the water's edge and stood just behind the troupe of monkeys, who were standing silently huddled together watching sadly as Charlie hauled Willy out of the water and laid him out on the bank.

Electrical sparks were emanating from various parts of his body, and an occasional wisp of ominous smoke drifted into the still air. Charlie knelt down and cradled Willy's head in his lap. He slowly opened his eyes, and a slight smile creased his scarecrow face. When he spoke, the voice was cracked and mechanical, and nothing like the ex-president's that had been built into him.

'Y...you really sh...should have made me w...waterproof, my maker.'

Charlie's head moved from side to side, in a desolate kind of way. 'It was the last thing on my mind when I made you, Willy. Then you ran away, so it was too late...'

'I...it doesn't matter, Ch...Charlie. I did g...good in the end, didn't I?'

Charlie tried not to show the devastation in his face. 'Don't try to speak, Willy. We'll get you back to the house, fix you up.'

A slightly-smoking hand curled weakly around his arm. 'With wh...what, Charlie? We b...both know the technology we need was d...destroyed in England. I can h...hardly go to hospital, c...can I?'

Charlie glanced around to his friends, desperately hoping one of them would suddenly experience a eureka moment. Danielle raised her hands from her sides, telling him what he already knew. Still he wasn't prepared to accept the inevitable.

'We could get you back to Norfolk, Willy. There's still some basic technology in Rupert's basement...'

Willy let out a final-sounding laugh. 'Charlie... it ain't g...gonna happen. It feels like I h...have seconds, not d...days.'

As if to emphasise his words, some kind of electrical short sparked a bigger flash from somewhere in his chest.

'Willy...'

'Accept it, my m...maker. I'm done for. I'm so s...sorry for you...'

'Sorry for me?'

'You're a g...genius, Charlie. Spent y...years creating me, and all for nothing. I'm a danger to the w... world, and the only place I couldn't d...do any harm was on an island so tiny n...no one even knew it existed.'

Charlie wiped away a tear with the back of his hand. 'Don't talk like that, Willy. Okay, the technology that created you was too dangerous to be hoisted on this world, but *you* were not.' He waved a hand at the tribe of monkeys watching on silently. 'Look at what you've done since you've been here. You're a changed man.'

Willy nodded his head, just about all he could manage to do. 'You called me a m...man, Charlie.'

'You are a man, Willy. A good man, and a... a friend.'

'Th...that means a lot. Will you do something f...for me, Charlie?'

'Whatever I can.'

'Find s...someone to take over the monkey school. They... they need their education.'

Charlie stroked Willy's face. 'That's the least I can do, Willy.'

The artificial eyes began to close. 'Th...thank you, my m...maker. I think it is time to say goodbye now.'

'Please, Willy...'

He gripped Charlie's arm a little tighter. 'Hey, take the p...positives from this. If it w...wasn't for me, you... you would never have met Danielle.'

Unable to keep her distance any longer, she ran to Willy and held him tight. His eyes opened a little wider. '*Oww*... mind the wounds.'

Charlie shook his head. 'Willy, we all know you don't feel pain, so stop being a drama queen.'

His face creased into a warm smile. 'I know you k...know. Just trying to lighten the situation...'

'Oh Willy...'

The eyes closed. His body jerked violently. Just before he expired, he managed a single, whispered sentence. *'Be safe... all of you...'*

His body went limp. And then, as if to make a point that didn't need making, an array of sparks sent a final wisp of deathly smoke into the air.

The tribe of monkeys seemed to expel a collective, desolate sigh. Daisy turned away, wrapping slightly-shaking hands around her head. 'Can this island get any more bizarre, Dip? Now I'm tearing up at the demise of an artificial intelligent being.'

Aidan wiped away his own mistiness, and pulled his wife close. 'Quite honestly, Flower, I don't think there's a dry eye in the jungle... human or monkey.'

She turned to him, and smiled through the tears. 'At least you and Su Shi are safe, dear. Now I worry about your brother. I think he got quite attached to his genius creation.'

'Wouldn't you?'

She nodded, and laid her head on his shoulder. 'I think I just discovered that I already have.'

Chapter 32

Charlie looked devastated. Still kneeling on the ground with Willy's head in his lap and Danielle's arms around his shoulders, not a sound broke the tragic silence.

Daisy looked at Aidan, and he nodded his unspoken agreement. They picked their way through the monkey tribe, and Aidan crouched down beside his brother.

'Charlie, we should get back to the house. I know this is devastating for us all, but we can't stay here forever.'

Charlie looked up to his brother, his eyes overflowing with tears. 'He was my life... until Danielle came along. And Willy hit the nail on the head, we never would have met if she hadn't been ordered to steal his technology. Now he's gone...'

'Bro, take some solace from the fact something good came out of this. I know Willy is a huge loss, both as a friend and as the last vestige of your genius, but he came good in the end. In a weird kind of way he did you proud.'

'I promised him we would keep the monkey school going. But I don't know how.'

Danielle glanced up to the tribe, still standing watching silently, some of them holding hands, sharing their grief. 'Hey guys... if Su Shi is willing, she and me will take over the school. If you folks agree, of course.'

In the background, Su Shi nodded her agreement. The tribe looked at each other, shaking and nodding their heads as they chatted amongst themselves to come to a collective decision. Then they let out toothy grins, and screeched their deafening approval.

Daisy smiled a resigned smile to Aidan. 'We have *got* to tell Maisie about this,' she said quietly.

'Careful... she'll probably believe you.'

The clearing fell silent. Aidan finally persuaded Charlie to make a move, after promising they would lay Willy respectfully in the log cabin until morning, when they'd fashion something to collect him for burial in his final resting place.

The monkeys said cheerio in their own way, and swung away through the trees. Aidan and Charlie carried Willy to the cabin, and laid him out gently onto the log bench. Then the four of them gathered in the small clearing. Danielle reached up to switch off the tripod lamp, which was still illuminating their little world thanks to the power from its own battery.

'Time to go home, guys,' she said quietly.

Her hand didn't quite reach the switch. From away in the distance, the sound of gunfire reverberated in the night air. Daisy looked towards the muffled sound. 'That's coming from somewhere out to sea. *Come on!*'

They thrashed their way through the dense undergrowth next to the inlet bank, the torches flashing as they hurried as fast as they could to the north shore. Luckily it was only a couple of hundred yards before they reached the rocky coastline.

Less than a mile offshore, something was going down. The pale moonlight was illuminating two vessels in the distance. One of them was in darkness, apart from the flashes of automatic gunfire. The other was easier to see, the powerful searchlight in the bows making it clear who was onboard.

As they watched, the beam picked out someone on the deck of the fishing boat. He wasn't on the deck for long. A shot rang out from the police patrol boat, and he crashed into the water.

'Let's hope that was the guy who shot Willy,' said Aidan emotionally.

More shots echoed across the water, the pirates not giving up the fight that could have only one ending. Then, that ending began to play out. A small explosion lit up the sky towards the rear of the fishing boat. As it began to sink, several pirates jumped for their lives into the sea.

A dark figure appeared on deck, a gun in her defiant hands. Daisy squinted to try and see better. *'Is that a woman?'*

Aidan nodded. 'Her name is Carla. She's the leader of the gang. Somehow I didn't think she'd go quietly.'

She must have known resistance was futile. For a reason unknown to her, she had no intention of being caught alive. That didn't quite work. Someone fired a single retaliatory shot, and she crumpled to the deck.

She wasn't dead. She struggled to her feet, staggering as the police boarded the sinking ship and dragged her away to their own. One minute later the fishing boat tipped onto its tail, and in seconds disappeared to the bottom of the sea.

A small inflatable boat sped to rescue the three men still alive in the water, and fished them out into captivity. Three minutes later the powerful engines of the patrol boat rose to a guttural growl, and it sped away in a north-westerly direction.

Charlie ran and hand through his hair. 'That's something I suppose.'

Aidan wrapped an arm around his shoulders. 'It's a strange kind of justice, Bro. The police obviously knew roughly where the pirates were all along, they were just waiting for them to show themselves.'

Su Shi took Charlie's hand. 'It is over, my friend. Not without loss, but perhaps we should thank our lucky stars and monkeys that the rest of us are still alive. I think now it really is time to leave this jungle and head back to the house.'

'I can't agree more,' said Daisy quietly, and a little shakily.

Chapter 33

Aidan leant on his spade and stretched his back, grateful their task was done. 'Phew, I'm not used to digging in this heat.'

Charlie found a smile. '*We* are... we seem to have spent half our time here digging up overgrowth, and then planting new stuff.'

'But look at what you guys have achieved.'

Charlie handed his brother a bottle of water. 'Maybe. Things will be different from now on though. One less of us to run around.'

Aidan took a swig of the water, and tried to smile reassuringly to his brother. 'Charlie, I know you lost a friend as well as half a lifetime's work, but we all owe it to Willy to carry on. He was working hard on this place after all. I mean, it is beautiful, isn't it?'

The two men were digging a deep grave in the ground next to the schoolhouse Willy had built. Aidan was right, it was a beautiful spot. Close to the shore on the eastern tip of the island, the three-sided schoolhouse with its palm-leaf roof looked just like a rustic building in the Caribbean should.

Sheltered on two sides by clumps of dense palm trees, it had been protected from the full force of hurricane Madeline, and had escaped virtually unscathed. It was an idyllic spot, and would remain a major part of Willy's legacy.

It was also the only location they could consider for his final resting place.

Daisy and Su Shi appeared. Straightaway Daisy noticed the strain on Aidan's face, and knew it wasn't just because of his toil in the midday sun.

'Us girls have finished the coffin... well, more of a coconut-wood box I suppose. But it looks fine enough,' she said to both men. Then she took Aidan's hand and turned him away. 'This is bringing back memories I guess, hey dear?'

He nodded sadly. 'No fooling you, huh?'

'I have known you a little while now.'

He lifted his eyes to the sky. 'I will confess I never expected the Willy saga to end with me burying someone again.'

'Sad memories.'

He squeezed her hand. 'It was hard enough burying Irina in Thetford Forest so no one would ever find her. That was at the start of the Willy era, and now at the end of it I'm helping bury him too... so no one will ever find him either.'

'It's hard, I know. And I also know I don't need to say this, but spare a thought for Charlie. He's not only burying someone who became a friend, but he's also saying a final goodbye to the technology he created. There's no way back for it now.'

He nodded his agreement. 'It's a wrench for him, even though he always knew this fragile world wasn't ready for such technology. In a way I know I'm not the only one who sees the irony. I think Charlie appreciates that despite how tragic it is, it is the final nail in the coffin that makes sure what he created will never fall into the wrong hands.'

'Aptly put, dear. If not exactly subtle.'

Su Shi called out. 'Danielle is making some lunch, so we should head back to the house. Then we will go collect Willy, and have the ceremony.'

Five humans and fifty monkeys gathered at the graveside. As Charlie stepped up to say a few words, the sun was just sinking behind the treetops in the west, bringing the traumatic day to its close.

He cleared his throat as Danielle took his hand. *'Be brave, darling,'* she whispered.

He nodded slowly, and began to speak.

'Willy, I will confess when I first made you, you were... well, a pain in my butt. It wasn't you, despite the fact I gave you the wrong character. It was what you represented. A technology so advanced and so dangerous I soon came to the conclusion I couldn't unleash you on the world.

'The fact you had other ideas caused a series of events that could well have been classified as catastrophic, if not for the intervention of some of those here today, and well, frankly, pure chance. Afterwards you told me you needed to die, and asked me to make it happen. That was when I realised you had exceeded your programming, to coin a phrase, and had begun to develop your own much more compassionate character.

'I refused to let you die, precisely because of that. We came here to this tiny island, and your new character grew ever more defined. Now we only need to look around to see how much you are going to be missed.'

The assembled tribe chattered their agreement.

'In the final act you died at the hands of someone who clearly couldn't handle the fact artificial life forms could be just as intelligent, and just as caring, as humans... and monkeys of course. Which, ironically, is one of the reasons we hid you from the world. So now we lay you to rest next to the place you made your own, as a tribute to the things you achieved in the face of considerable odds. Yes Willy, you did make a positive difference, and you touched the hearts of every one of us here today.

'And so we say a final goodbye, not just to a good friend, but also to a brand new life-form, who was perhaps always destined to be too volatile for the world to handle. That wasn't your fault, and in many ways you became an innocent victim of your own success. Goodbye my friend, and be at peace, knowing you will always be in the hearts of your friends. Love and respect to you, in every way.'

Charlie lowered his head, and then wiped away a tear. Danielle pulled him close, and held him tight as Su Shi threw a posy of tropical flowers onto the top of the coffin. For a few seconds no one moved. All was silent, but then someone else ambled up to the graveside.

The monkey who seemed to be the head of the tribe held out the sergeant's cap he'd been wearing in the jungle. With a sobby kind of smile, Charlie took it. *'Thank you, my friend,'* he whispered.

The monkey glanced to the coffin, and then back to the hat in Charlie's hands, making sure his human friend knew what he would like to see. Charlie nodded, and dropped the cap onto the top of the coffin.

The monkey students let out a collective cry, which sounded more like a lament. Daisy turned away, shaking her head at her own emotional overload. 'For god's sake dear, bury that coffin before I burst into uncontrollable tears,' she mumbled.

All five of them shovelled the earth over the coffin, as quickly as they could. Finally the grave was filled, and Su Shi placed a plain wooden plaque at its head. They wanted to mark it properly but, tiny island or not, they'd agreed they couldn't run the risk of strangers one day finding it, and unearthing the technology that needed to stay buried forever.

They said their brief last respects, and then began the walk back to the house as the gloom of a beautiful evening finally began to turn to night. At the top of the slight ridge, just before they were out of sight of the compound, Daisy glanced back. It stopped her in her tracks.

'Well, would you look at that,' she said in an awe-inspired kind of way.

The others turned to look back. Aidan let out a tiny cry. The monkeys had returned, all fifty of them, gathered silently at the graveside. Sitting motionless on their haunches, they were paying their own respects with a vigil to their much-loved head teacher.

'Well, that's a sight that will stay with me until the day I die,' said Charlie quietly.

Danielle slipped her hand into his. 'I'll make sure it will. And if what I suspect is true, they won't leave until the light of morning.'

Chapter 34

Aidan took his wife's hand at the breakfast table. 'I know we got sidetracked by events we never anticipated, dear, but now we have to focus on the real reason we came. We've already been here longer than we'd hoped.'

'Just getting my brain around it now, Dip. It's a bit hard, after what happened.'

'The world is full of surprises, hey Flower?'

'Yes. And not all of them nice ones.'

She glanced across to Charlie, still looking like his own world had been smashed to pieces at his feet. In a way, it kind of had. He shook his head sadly, and almost mumbled the words. 'I really should have made Willy waterproof.'

Aidan tried to pull his brother out of the depression. 'He still got hit by two slugs, Charlie. With no technology anymore to fix him up, he likely wouldn't be here now anyway. Speaking bluntly, the water was just one part of his demise. I doubt even if you'd made him waterproof the outcome would have been any different.'

Charlie switched the shake to a nod. 'Thanks, Bro. I guess you're right. It just feels like the end of an era, you know?'

Daisy felt she had to say something else, which was likely just as blunt. 'We all feel the same, Charlie, but we also know it's harder for you than any of the rest of us. Willy was your baby, even though there's an argument to say that he never should have been born in the first place.'

He found a weak smile. 'He knew that too, after we left Thetford Forest. When I was fixing his arm back in Rupert's basement he said he wanted to die, because he was a ticking time bomb that was better off not existing. I refused to terminate him, because the character I made sure he inherited would never have said such a thing, and I realised then he was changing of his own volition.'

Aidan nodded his agreement. 'Indeed... and his time on this island just proved how much he had changed.'

'Beyond recognition,' Daisy added.

Charlie stood up, and lifted his hands from his sides. 'I suppose I wanted to see where he would take himself, despite his original character still resurfacing on occasions. Now we won't get the chance.'

Daisy stood up too, and placed a consoling hand on his arm. 'I think we did get the chance, Charlie. Perhaps nowhere near as long a chance as you wanted, but in just over a year Willy left his mark, and proved beyond doubt he was a new man.'

Thanks, Daisy. That means a lot.'

Daisy looked pointedly at Su Shi. Unwilling to spent the night mourning alone in the lodge, she'd stayed at the main house. 'Su Shi, we need to get your mind back to the original reason we came. The truth is...'

'Aidan told me, while we were in captivity. I do not think I have anything that can help clear your name though.'

Daisy screwed up her her face. 'I guess we always thought it was a long shot. Last chance saloon, and all that?'

'You have been so good to me, all of you. The least I can do is come back to Norfolk with you, and tell that obnoxious man what I know about nineteen-ninety-eight and earlier this year. Testify for you.'

'And then what? Get the electric chair for your so-called crimes?'

'They do not allow capital punishment in the UK, Daisy.'

'And that means you'll stay living?'

Su Shi's eyes dropped to the floor. 'Perhaps I will.'

Aidan spoke firmly. 'No you won't, and you know it. If a covert Chinese hit-squad doesn't get you, someone else will. Thanks for the offer, but we can't allow that. You're safe and comfortable on this island, and that's the way it's going to stay.'

'Daisy, please...'

'Sorry. I'm with Aidan on that one.'

'But I do not see how else I can help. I need to help.'

'Is there nothing... no documents or anything from back then?'

She shook her head in a frustrated kind of way. 'No. I still have most of the diaries I kept from when I was a little girl, but I stopped writing them about ten years ago. What I was doing was getting too depressing to keep reminding myself of.'

'Does one of the diaries go back to ninety-eight?'

'Yes, but remember I was a small girl then. I didn't really know much about what was going on until years after my father was killed, and I became determined to find out who was involved in his death.'

'Nevertheless, there might be something useful in the diaries. I realise such things are personal, but would you mind if we go through them together?'

'Of course not, when there is the vague possibility that something might help.'

Danielle went with them to the lodge, and while Su Shi found the diaries she made them all coffees. Then they sat together around the small table, and spread the diaries out on the top.

'Wow, there's a lot of them,' said Aidan.

'Then the sooner we make a start, the sooner we'll know whether there's anything useful here or not,' said Daisy. 'May we?'

Su Shi nodded, and opened the ninety-eight year. 'It is in Chinese, written when I was a child and did not speak very much English. When I grew up, the later diaries are in English.'

'Maybe you should go through the Chinese ones, while we delve into the more recent years. Look for anything that might give us leverage to shoot Mildew's suppositions down.'

'There will not be anything in these older ones. I was just a child. If there is anything you can use it will be in the later years.'

'Let's get snooping... in the most respectful of ways of course.'

Chapter 35

For two hours they poured through Su Shi's diaries. The years written as she grew into a woman, hiding in the mountains of North China being intensively trained by her Triad family, made harrowing reading.

Eventually Daisy and Aidan had to give their emotions a break, so told the others they needed some fresh air, and took their fifth coffees outside. Sitting on the terrace, Daisy exhaled a fraught breath.

'This is difficult reading, Dip. So much hatred in her words.'

'Yes. Perhaps justified hatred though. She grew up in a divided world, where hatred was part of life.'

'I suppose you can understand it from her point of view. She was just a child when the father she loved was taken from her.'

'By people who knew exactly what they were doing.'

'And people who ended up paying for it.'

'From quite an early age she swore to take revenge on those who had deliberately sacrificed her father for their own ends. I'm now working through the years where almost every page details who she took her retaliation on, and how.'

'You have to admire her, in a strange kind of way though. Talk about single-minded.'

Daisy threw her gaze to the Caribbean sky. 'Once her Triad family knew how determined she was they trained her up to be equipped to take revenge. In a way they encouraged her, and turned her into the feared assassin who became known as the Shanghai Shadow. It was only when we met in the Lake District she eventually admitted she'd had enough.'

'And yet through all those dark years she was meticulous, and didn't do anything too crazy. She spent a long time researching the people responsible, and only when she was sure, made them pay.'

Daisy nodded sadly. 'It's to her credit that somehow she maintained enough of her own character to realise revenge can only go so far before it consumes you completely.'

Aidan slipped a hand into his wife's. 'I realise that had started to happen before you two met, but it was still down to you she made the final transition from the Shanghai Shadow to just plain Su Shi.'

Daisy chuckled mirthlessly. 'Even though I almost killed her for what she did to Sarah.'

'But you didn't. Perhaps like her you understood people can actually change.'

'I think we're perhaps more alike than I care to admit.'

Aidan nodded his agreement, but didn't voice it out loud. 'We'd better go back and carry on our difficult reading, dear.'

Just before two they broke for lunch. There were only a few diaries still to go through, but none of them had given up anything that could help exonerate Daisy.

Both she and Alex had been mentioned briefly, short notes that Su Shi's research had revealed neither was guilty of doing anything treasonous, or being guilty of warning bin Laden of the missile strike.

It was little comfort. Even if they took that particular diary back to England, the written word of an assassin wanted in more than one country would hold no weight in court. All that would happen is that they'd be forced to admit how they'd come across it, and when both refused to answer that would be the end of everything regardless.

Deliberately withholding information would be seen as an admission of guilt.

Even if they allowed Su Shi to return to England with them, her testimony would have the same effect, and then some. If she even managed to get to court before the SIS banged her up, anything she said would be ripped to shreds as unreliable by the prosecution.

Then they'd have to explain what happened in the Lake District. As far as MI6 was concerned the organisation was never involved. Despite Daisy doing most of what they asked of her she was 'officially' acting on her own, and in addition aiding and abetting a wanted criminal to disappear off the face of the Earth... a crime in itself.

Whichever way Daisy and Aidan came at it, it wasn't looking good.

They reached the end of the diaries, already realising they were on a losing wicket. They'd always known the only way the journals could have helped was if some kind of exonerating event had been contained in the words they could investigate quickly, or someone was mentioned who could have spoken up for Daisy.

There was nothing, and no one.

Most of those mentioned in the entries were there because they no longer existed.

Aidan sat back, and covered his face with his hands. Daisy put a hand on his arm. 'It's okay, Dip. We always knew it was a long shot anyway.'

'It's not okay though, is it?' he spat back. 'We only just survived a hurricane out at sea, then ended up spending our time tackling pirates in a jungle, Willy lost his life... and it's all for nothing.'

She leant over and held him tight. 'Hey. Dip. It's not been for nothing. Danielle and Charlie might not have come out of it so well if it hadn't been for the rest of us.'

Danielle stood up from the table, and wrapped her arms around the two of them. 'Daisy's right. If we hadn't gone to find Su Shi and her diaries that morning we would never have known about our temporary inhabitants. They would likely have found us first, and then I hate to think what would have happened...'

He tried to smile. 'I know. I'm sorry. I just wish...'

'I wish too, Aidan. I wish there was something we could do. I just don't know what. We've been through the diaries with a toothcomb, and there's no mention of anything or anyone that could help.'

Su Shi looked devastated. 'I am sorry. I am afraid my diaries were an indication of my single-minded mission in life. Do you see now why I stopped writing them?'

'It's not your fault, Su Shi. I don't think there's a single person on this planet who can help us now.'

Danielle nodded slowly. 'You can say that again. According to the list I briefly scanned, most of the names have been crossed off because they're either already dead or weren't responsible for any misdeeds in ninety-eight. Like you, Daisy.'

'Um... list?'

'Sure. I didn't take a lot of notice of it. It was in the back of one of the diaries I read through.'

Su Shi explained. 'It was the original list I made, just after I started my research. It noted everyone who was, or might have been involved in my father's death. During a five year period the list grew longer. Then I began to cross out names as I eliminated those who I discovered were undoubtedly at fault, and a few others who I found out were innocent, and then I made a digital copy of it. That was the list Alex discovered online. I did not even realise the old paper list was still in that diary.'

'May I see it?' said Daisy.

Danielle sorted through the random pile of diaries on the table. 'Yes, this is the one... I think.' She opened the journal at the back. The scruffy old piece of paper fell out. 'There you go,' she said as she handed it to Daisy.

'Wow... it's a long list,' said Daisy as she unfolded it.

'I discovered a lot of people had fingers in a very murky pie,' said Su Shi.

'Hmm... a lot of them at the top appear to be Chinese,' said Daisy as she began to scan it. 'And crossed out.'

'That is because my own country was the first place I started researching. A lot of them are dead because they deliberately sent my father into a dangerous situation,' Su Shi said matter-of-factly.

Daisy scanned through the list. Then her eyes opened wide, and her hands began to shake. *Well, well, well,'* she whispered.

'Dear?'

She held out the list so Su Shi could see. 'Why is that name crossed out?

'Ah, I remember. It was suspicious at first, but I could never prove or disprove guilt so thought no more about it.'

'I see.'

'Dear..?'

She handed to list to Aidan with a grin, and tapped the relevant place with a finger. Aidan's eyes opened even wider than Daisy's had.

'Well, well, well...' he said.

Daisy and Aidan sat up in bed that night, drinking tea once again. It was their last night in the Caribbean. Getting back to Norfolk quickly had become a priority.

'Don't get too excited, dear,' said Aidan, noticing the sparkle was back in his wife's eyes. 'Su Shi said there was no proof either way against that name. It might be nothing.'

'It doesn't matter.'

'Huh?'

'At least we were lucky there's a military flight back from Cumaná tomorrow afternoon. Charlie and Danielle have offered to take us to the airbase in their boat, which is a damn site safer and faster than the one we came on.'

'Seven hours as opposed to twelve,' said Aidan. 'And not so much likelihood of the captain jumping ship, or of ramming a beach in Trinidad.'

Daisy chuckled. 'And no possibility of falling foul of a hurricane either.'

Aidan took a sip of his tea. 'So come on, what do you mean, "it doesn't matter"? Morbid Mildew is about to turn up on our doorstep with a warrant, so we're not going to have time to do the research Su Shi didn't, even if it's possible after all this time.'

'As I said, it doesn't matter.'

'Dear, please stop being so infuriatingly mysterious.'

Daisy turned to him and smiled. 'We've discovered enough to make it happen regardless, Dip. Or not happen, more to the point.'

'But... but there's no proof...'

'Who needs proof? Think about dear Eric. He doesn't have any *real* evidence of my guilt, just supposition. That doesn't make any difference to him.'

'Don't tell me you're...'

She tapped him on the arm, and then kissed him on the cheek. 'Ever heard of calling someone's bluff, dear?'

'Oh my god... that's a dangerous game in these circumstances.'

'I know. But *these circumstances* are exactly why we have to play that particular game, dear.'

'I suppose if anyone can pull it off it's you.'

'Believe it. And now we need sleep. We've got an early cruise in the morning.'

Aidan switched off the light and spooned his wife, not as all sure if he would actually manage to find any sleep.

Chapter 36

Celia answered the phone. She groaned as the voice introduced itself, despite the fact she'd been expecting the call.

'Good morning, Miss Henderson. Eric Mildew here. It seems your mother and father are still not answering their phones, so I assume they are not yet back from their dead zone in, um... Cornwall?'

'You assume correctly. At least I haven't heard from them.' Jack appeared next to Celia, so she switched the phone to speaker.

'How surprising. You need to be informed I have now obtained a court warrant, to empower me to search both your premises and those of your mother's.'

'Feeling chipper then?' said Celia sarcastically.

'I'm sorry?'

Well you can't search Fern Cottage if they're not there.'

'Oh but I can, Miss Henderson. If there is no one home, I can force entry.'

'Don't you dare.'

'Please don't test me. Unless you possess a key, I will force entry.'

Celia glanced to Jack, who nodded silently. 'Okay, we have a key. But this is an infringement of our privacy.'

'I can assure you in these circumstances, privacy is out of the window. Which luckily I don't have to gain entry by.' He chuckled annoyingly at his own joke.

'So when can we expect the pleasure of your company?'

'One hour. I will visit you first, and execute the first stage of the warrant.'

'One hour? I'm not even dressed yet.'

'Then I suggest you put on some clothes. One hour, no longer.'

Celia slammed the phone down. Jack couldn't stop a grin. 'He sounds even more like Inspector Mallory over the phone.'

'It's not funny. I'm starting to feel as flustered as Mrs. McCarthy.'

'I'm surprised you didn't tell him to stuff his warrant up his...'

'Oh sure. Refusing to allow the authorities to execute a warrant is a criminal offence. That's hardly going to do mum much good is it? Or the Henderson Detective Agency, come to that.'

He pulled her into his arms. 'Hey, we've got nothing to hide. Well you have, unless you go and get dressed.'

She found a smile, and thumped him playfully. 'I'm calling Sarah first.'

'Sarah? Why?'

'Because if she's available I'd like her here. An official observer, just in case.'

'You really don't want the police to see you thumping an MI6 agent though.'

'Promise I'll behave. But if you see a fist starting to clench, just grab it quick.'

'Oh, I will.'

Celia picked up the phone. 'Where the hell is mum and dad anyway?'

'No idea. Except for the fact they're definitely not in Cornwall.'

Sarah arrived five minutes before Mildew. Celia found a smile as she walked in. 'Wow, look at you, all doled up in your sergeant's stripes.'

Sarah gave her a twirl. 'Do they suit me?'

'They would have suited you months ago. Long overdue.'

Sarah smiled, but it didn't last longer than a second. 'So what do you want me to do?

'Nothing. Just be here, looking pretty and official. I want Mildew to know we're taking this seriously, and if he steps out of line we've got a credible witness.'

'And what about if *you* step out of line, mother's daughter and all that?'

Celia chuckled. 'I've already asked Jack to restrain me if I try anything Daisy-esque.'

'Wise. They're still not back from, um, Cornwall I take it?'

'Still no sign, so we're on our own.'

'Not for much longer, I very much doubt.'

Sarah's words were well founded. The kettle had only just boiled when the front door was gently hammered. Celia opened it.

'Mr. Mildew. How delightful to see you.'

He tipped his bowler, in a sarcastic kind of way. 'Likewise.' He held out the warrant like a little child holding out money for an ice cream. 'I assume you'd like to check this?'

Celia batted it away. 'No need. You're hardly likely to pull the same trick twice, are you? You'd better come in.'

As he walked into the living room Jack looked up in surprise. 'Ah, Mildew. Um... no posse of men in much more up-to-date black suits?'

Eric shook his head, almost like he was expecting such a remark. 'No, just me. As I informed your mother, MI6 is rather stretched right now.' He caught sight of Sarah. 'Ah, I see you have involved the police. A pointless exercise, but I suppose I might have expected such a move.'

Sarah threw him an insulted glare. 'Are you saying I'm pointless, Mr. Mildew?'

For a second he looked uncomfortable. 'Um, no, of course not. This search will be conducted according to the laws of the United Kingdom. There is no need for a police presence, that's all.'

'Really? A search conducted by a single person? We might be here some time.'

'As I said... oh, never mind. Shall we just get on with it, please?'

'Be my guest,' said Celia.

'You may accompany me, if you so wish.'

Jack waved a hand at the man. 'Just get on with it. We have nothing to hide.'

'Very well.'

Mildew disappeared up the stairs. Celia looked at Sarah. 'This is odd. A search warrant, executed by a team of one?'

Sarah nodded. 'We would never conduct a search solo... but then again I've not been involved in one carried out by MI6.'

Jack seemed to agree with Celia. 'Hmm... stretched resources or not, it does seem a bit weird. Maybe we'd better make some lunch. We'll have plenty of time to kill.'

There wasn't plenty of time to kill. Ten minutes after Mildew had disappeared up the stairs, he was back again at the foot of them. 'Now, if you will please take me to Fern Cottage.'

'*What?* You're done already? What about the kitchen, and the office? Don't you want to appropriate our computer or something?'

'Um... that won't be necessary. And please don't tell me how to do my job.' Then, just to prove he was doing his job, he poked his head around the kitchen door and scanned the room for a full five seconds. 'We're done here. Fern Cottage, *now* please?'

A wide-eyed Celia, Jack and Sarah piled into Sarah's police car for the very short journey to Daisy and Aidan's cottage. There was just time for Celia to form a single sentence, in a somewhat incredulous tone. 'What the hell is going on? *That* was an executed search warrant?'

'Beats me,' said Jack.

At the kitchen door, Celia turned to Mildew. 'My mother isn't going to be too pleased about this.'

He grinned menacingly, and a little nauseatingly. 'Indeed she won't. She's also not likely to be pleased when I inform her the case is to be passed to the Crown Prosecution Service in the morning, with a recommendation to proceed to conviction for several serious crimes.'

'You really are a joy to behold, aren't you, Mildew?'

'Just doing my job.'

The four of them walked into the kitchen, three of them more reluctantly than the fourth. 'Another ten minute search, Mildew?' said Celia sarcastically.

He glared at her like a headmaster about to whip out his cane. 'I'll thank you to keep your remarks to yourself, Miss Henderson. How I do my job, and how long I take doing it, is my concern.'

'You know best,' said Celia, equally sarcastically.

'Yes, well... I'll start upstairs. Would you like to accompany me this time, sergeant?'

'Not really. Just be aware if I find anything an inch out of place I shall be informing my DCI.'

'Oh, I'm sure you will.'

He began to head for the passageway leading to the staircase, but didn't get any further. Instead he looked round in shock as a stern voice rang out from the kitchen door.

'What the bloody hell are you doing in my house?'

Chapter 37

'Mum, dad... you're back... from Cornwall.'

'Yes, it would appear we are,' said Daisy curtly, locking her stare into Morbid Mildew.

'We weren't quite expecting a reception committee though,' said Aidan, equally curtly.

'Guys, I'm sorry... Mildew turned up with a search warrant, and we didn't want him forcing entry...'

'It's okay, Celia dear. It saves us calling him, and requesting a visit.'

'Mum?'

'Mr. Mildew and I have some business, don't we Eric?'

Eric looked a little uneasy, maybe because his Daisy-free ride had been disturbed. Still he seemed quite prepared to bluster his way through his business. 'Indeed we do. Not that it directly concerns you right now.'

'Oh, I think it does.'

Aidan held out an arm. 'May I see this search warrant please, Mr. Mildew?'

A hesitant hand passed it to him. He and Daisy studied it together. 'It looks genuine enough,' said Daisy.

'Of course it's genuine...' Mildew protested.

'What do you think, dear?' said Daisy.

'I find it grossly offensive,' said Aidan, a slight grin on his face.

'Me too,' said Daisy, and then tore it into four pieces.

Morbid Mildew imploded, his face reddening with anger in the space of a single second. 'Good god, woman... that's the property of MI6 you're defacing...'

'Coffee, Mr. Mildew? Jack dear, please put the kettle on. It looks like our guest could do with a strong one.'

'I don't want a bloody coffee. I intend to carry out my search, despite the fact you have deliberately destroyed official papers.'

'Please sit down, Mr. Mildew. As I said, we have matters to discuss.'

'I'm not ruddy well sitting down.' He turned away, and stomped towards the staircase.

'*I said sit*. Please?'

He stopped stomping. 'Well really. I shall be reporting this to my superiors.' Then his face changed, as something occurred to him. 'Unless this concerns you wishing to confess of course?'

'In your dreams.'

'I thought as much.' He turned again in the direction of the stairs, until Celia caught his arm. 'I think if you know what's good for you, Mr. Mildew, you should sit down and hear what my parents have to say, before...'

'Before what?'

'Before my mother does something we will all regret. She is a little... unstable, after all.'

Daisy, who in different circumstances wouldn't have let that go without some kind of witty retort, decided it would be more suitable to smile sweetly. 'Shall we all sit down and relax?'

'Relax?' The red-faced man started to protest, then glanced around at the hostile stares of everyone else present, caved in and did as Daisy asked. While Jack busied himself making coffee, the rest of them took their seats in the living area. Everyone made sure they sat in a semi-circle around Morbid Mildew, ensuring there was no doubt he was the centre of attention, whether he liked it or not.

On the flight home, Daisy and Aidan had used their time to formulate a strategy. Largely based on bluff, they'd anticipated a little more time to brief the others on the staged final act that would have played out when they were ready. That wasn't now going to happen.

Finding a reception committee the moment they reached home wasn't part of the plan, but it wouldn't have to matter. The curtain had already risen, so now all they had to do was ad lib to the best of their ability, without the star of the production realising they were.

Aidan glanced around at the lack of Mildew allies. 'Correct me if I'm wrong, Mr. Mildew, but aren't search warrants usually executed with a lot more personnel?'

'I... we're extremely stretched at the moment, so I had to go solo. Not that it's any business of yours.'

Daisy smiled sweetly again. 'I think perhaps it is.'

'You're not making any sense... as usual.'

'Throwing out insults won't get you anywhere, Mr. Mildew,' said Aidan, turning the obnoxious man's words on their heads.

'Get me anywhere? You do realise my investigations are virtually complete? This house search is the final box I need to tick, and then your wife will be charged with treason, murder, and aiding a wanted criminal to escape.'

'That sounds like a serious list of offences,' said Daisy, a finger on the chin.

'Of course it is. And there's no escape.'

'I see.'

'Um... pardon me for my observations, but you don't exactly seem to be consumed by abject guilt?'

Daisy let out a deliberate chuckle. 'So, you say executing this search warrant is the final box you need to tick?'

'Do I have to say it twice?'

'Just confirming what you said. It's a terrible shame you won't get to tick it then.'

Chapter 38

Jack handed the open-jawed man a coffee. He took it with a hand shaking with anger, and then spluttered out a protest.

'*I beg your pardon?* You forfeited the right to make decisions off your own bat when you committed these crimes.'

Aidan shot him down. 'So you're telling my wife she can't do what she wants in her own home?'

'No... no, but...'

'But nothing, Mr. Mildew. I suggest you shut your mouth and listen to what we have to say.'

'I...' He shut his mouth, realising it was the best option he had right then.

Daisy leant back in the chair, trying to appear in command, like all the best interrogators do. 'So Eric, I assume you've been with the Secret Intelligence Service some time?'

'What the hell has that got to do with anything?'

'Answer the question please, before I whip out my shotgun.'

The mouth dropped open, before it closed again, and then reopened to answer the question he had little option but to answer. 'I... yes, many years.'

'Hmm... many years. And yet you are still a relatively minor senior official?'

'I... I refused to kowtow to my superiors just to obtain promotion, if you must know.'

'So you were overlooked, on more than one occasion then?'

'That's none of your business.'

'I think it is my mother's business right now,' said Celia, tuning in to the fact there were revelations in the wind.

Aidan took up the grilling. 'And now you have been supposedly put in charge of trawling through old, dead cases... just on the offchance you might find a morsel of impropriety lurking somewhere.'

'*Well, really...* it's a responsible job. And there's no *supposedly* about it either.'

Daisy smiled sympathetically. 'Do forgive my husband, Eric. He can possess an acid tongue at times.'

Several raised eyebrows aimed themselves at Daisy, but no one said anything out loud.

She ignored them. 'However, he does raise a relevant point. There would seem to be a case for assuming your tiny, lonely office in the basement was, at best, a sideways promotion?'

'That's your opinion.'

'Perhaps. But we are now wondering why it happened.'

Aidan let out a chuckle. 'Maybe something unfortunate occurred, dear?'

'Did something unfortunate happen, Eric?'

'I... there was never any proof... just tongues wagging...'

'Ah, I see. So when precisely did you begin your career in my beloved MI6, Eric?'

'I don't see...'

'*When*, please?'

He stood up suddenly. 'I'm leaving now. Be assured this atrocity will be reported to the relevant authorities.'

Sarah stood in his way. 'Like me, Mr. Mildew?'

'Um...'

She thrust her hands on her hips. 'Officially I cannot see any misdemeanours being committed here. All I am observing is several people having a chat over coffee. Is that a crime in MI6 circles now, Mr. Mildew?'

'Well, no...'

'Then I suggest you sit, and finish your coffee.'

'You're in league with them, aren't you?'

'Then report me for having a personal connection to the case.'

'Oh I will, trust me,' he muttered, but then sat down anyway.

Daisy smiled gratefully to Sarah. 'So Eric, *when did you begin your career at MI6?*'

'Ninety-two,' he said in a small voice.

And how long until you did any more than make tea?'

'Um... three years. That damned organisation doesn't recognise talent when they see it.'

'And which department were you then seconded to?'

The answer took a moment to come. 'Terrorism, specifically in the Arab states.'

'I see. So you were unhappy with your slow career progress, for which you blamed others, and likewise the salary that you felt was an insult to the work you did?'

'I still don't see what this has got to do with anything.'

'Really?'

'So I was a bitter young man, taken advantage of at every turn. I'm not now.'

Aidan shook his head. 'No, perhaps you are not. Now you aim your bitterness at others. I wonder why?'

'What do you mean by that?' said Eric, starting to squirm uncomfortably, which gave everyone a clue he knew exactly what was meant.

Daisy, starting to realise their bluff was paying dividends, deliberately turned the screw. 'So I'm assuming then you were hovering around in the MI6 background in ninety-eight?'

'I was vaguely aware of what was going down, yes.'

'I think you were more than vaguely aware, Eric. If I'm not very much mistaken it was you who warned Osama bin Laden where and when an attempt on his life was to happen.'

Chapter 39

For a full ten seconds it seemed like the power of speech had left him. Then he found it again, out of sheer desperation. 'You're insane. This is just an attempt to deflect away from your own guilt.'

Aidan grinned annoyingly, from Morbid Mildew's point of view anyway. 'Ah, that's interesting. Correct me if I'm wrong, but isn't *deflection* what this is all about? You found yourself in a windowless basement room, given the unenviable task of trawling through cold cases that none of your bosses ever thought would see the light of day again. In recent times Putin's Russia has got aggressive once more, and so has China. If our guess is right, you were given a new task of making sure there were no comebacks that might embarrass MI6 relating to those countries or their allies... like Afghanistan.'

Daisy took up the accusations she actually had no proof of. 'You realised your past secret life would be exposed if you delved too deeply like you were told. You couldn't take the risk, so instead you ran to your bosses like a child telling tales, saying you'd discovered evidence I was the one who'd sold her country out. It's quite clever, if a little... classic.'

Mildew fidgeted even more uncomfortably, and then spluttered out a shot that flew well wide of the target. 'I... that's... that's just supposition. It'll never stand up in court.'

'No, I know it won't. If MI6 didn't find any evidence you were a Taliban sympathiser years ago, no one will find it now. I assume that's why you got demoted to the basement, because they suspected you were a double-agent but had no proof. They couldn't sack you or prosecute without evidence, so you were relegated somewhere you could do no harm. Am I right?'

'I... you're just assuming again,' Eric stammered, looking like he was silently pleading for a sink hole to open up and swallow him.

'Actually we're not. We've been to see someone who knew the truth, and who told us all we needed to know. Hence the reason you're now crapping yourself.'

'I'm not... I haven't... who?'

'Sorry, I'm not at liberty to say. So how much did they pay you?'

'Um... I'm not at liberty to say.'

'No real surprise there.'

Aidan laid out the deal. 'I suggest you formally drop all charges against my wife, Mr. Mildew, and we'll forget any of this ever happened.'

Daisy leant forward. 'We hate making deals with double agents, Eric, but in this case my freedom is more important than any justice. So I suggest you scuttle off with your tail between your legs, and when you get back to London you tender your formal resignation from the service. I can't imagine anyone will be too unhappy to see you go.'

'And what if I don't?'

Sarah stood up, and stretched as tall as her slight frame would allow. 'If you don't, then you will be formally arrested for offences under the official secrets act... something which, in my humble opinion, should happen anyway.'

'It seems you've got my mum to thank for being let off the hook,' said Celia. 'But given how unstable she is, I can't promise how long you'll be let off the hook for. She does have a reputation for exacting revenge after all.'

'Yes dear, perhaps that's enough now.'

'Just making sure Eric here is aware of the situation, mum.'

'Oh, he's aware alright,' said Eric in a small voice.

'So we have a deal then?' said Aidan.

'I really don't have a choice, do I?'

'No you don't. As you might discover, my wife is a law unto herself, Mr. Mildew.'

Eric sucked in a few deep and shaky breaths, positioned his bowler hat onto his trembling head, stood up quickly and marched through the door with as much bravado as he could muster. Which wasn't a lot.

After a rapid and somewhat comical half-run along the path, he disappeared behind the hedge.

Never to be seen again.

Daisy slumped back into the armchair, and wafted a relieved hand across her face. 'Phew. That was a little fraught, dears.'

'Mum, you both played a blinder. So why do you look so relieved?'

'Um... maybe because we didn't know any hard facts for sure, dear.'

Jack dropped onto the sofa. 'So you called his bluff? Wasn't that a bit risky?'

Aidan nodded his head vigorously. 'Why do you think we're looking so breathless?'

'How the hell did you discover all that... in *Cornwall*?'

'Um... we didn't go to Cornwall, as I'm sure you are well aware. We discovered Mildew's name on Su Shi's hit list, but she'd crossed it out as she couldn't unearth anything to implicate him. So we had to... kind of improvise.'

'Su... you've been to Emerald Island? Wow, I hope you had a nice time.'

'Yes dear, it was...exhilarating.'

'You can say that again,' said Aidan.

Sarah looked like her wings had been clipped. 'You should still have let me arrest him. It would have looked good on my CV.'

'And what about me? Morbid Mildew is so bitter and twisted he could easily have retaliated by telling everything he knew about what happened earlier this year... the one time I did do a couple of things I actually could be prosecuted for.'

Sarah threw her hands in the air, still smarting. 'I suppose you have a point. But someone has got away with treasonous acts, which isn't sitting easy.'

Daisy put a hand on her arm. 'If I remember right, in January you let someone get away quite happily, despite the fact she'd committed acts which made her a wanted woman in a number of countries.'

'Well... that was different.'

'How?'

'Su Shi wasn't anywhere near as obnoxious, for one thing.'

Aidan laughed. 'So, Detective-Sergeant Lowry, you're letting your personal feelings get in the way of your professional judgement?'

Sarah smiled, although she really didn't want to. 'Okay, say it like it is, Aidan.'

Daisy pointed something out. 'You say *get away with it*, but Mildew has no choice now but to resign. At his age his professional life is over, and somehow I doubt he has lots of caring friends to support him. He's a sad man, who will only get sadder.'

'Poetic justice then, I suppose.'

Celia had a thought. 'You said Su Shi hadn't found anything incriminating on Mildew. Now he's actually incriminated himself, are you going to tell her he was the one who warned bin Laden?'

Daisy glanced to Aidan, who shook his head to agree with the unspoken question, and then answered her daughter. 'No, we're not. Her days as the Shanghai Shadow are in the past, and that's something I can relate to. Morbid Mildew has got his just desserts, so if we tell her he was the one responsible it might inflame old feelings. I think for her sake it is better to let sleeping dogs lie.'

'I agree. You guys still took a big risk though,' said Jack.

Daisy and Aidan let out collective sighs. 'Luckily it paid off. Now we need time to recover from the strain. There's a new bottle of brandy in the cupboard... would one of you crack it open please?'

Chapter 40

Two days later, Daisy and Aidan were preparing some lunch when they heard the sound of a car pulling into the drive. A minute later someone knocked the front door.

'Rupert. This is a surprise.'

'I didn't know if your phones were still tapped, although I don't think they are. I just wanted to see how you guys are doing. I have some news too.'

'You'd better come in then.'

Aidan handed him a coffee as he sat down. 'I assume it's good news?'

'I suppose if you look at it from your point of view it is.'

'Not from yours?'

'Letting a double agent off the hook never sits well, even after retirement.'

'Sarah said the same thing, but you must agree that, given what he knows about recent events, it's best for all of us.'

He let out a deep sigh. 'I can't argue with that. I was a little surprised when I got a call from the Mildenhall base commander asking for an extra round of golf, but then I realised there was good reason.'

'We asked him to arrange it so he could bring you up to speed in the wide open spaces of the golf course, away from snooping ears.'

'I realised that, so we played a round yesterday. I was a little surprised at what he told me.'

Daisy narrowed her eyes. 'You were climbing the MI6 ladder back when it all happened, so you must have known something was going on?'

'In truth he wasn't known to me. MI6 was a big place back then, and I was just a department manager. There were whispers he was a Taliban informer, but nothing was ever proved. But just to be sure, he was sidelined to somewhere he could do no harm.'

'Or so you thought.'

Rupert shook his head. 'Indeed. Fortunately we got away with more recent events, thanks to you guys and your double-bluff, as it were.'

'I think so. But Mildew could still go to the papers or something, out of sheer spite.'

'That won't happen.'

'How can you be so sure?'

'That's what I came to tell you. At close of play last night Eric Mildew resigned from the SIS, and told his boss he wouldn't be back.'

'Well, we assumed that would happen. We, um... kind of made sure it would.'

'Ah yes, but what you don't know is that this morning I called Clive Morrison, to ensure he understood the implications of situation too. Basically he's the only one in authority who knows what happened in the Lake District.'

Daisy chuckled. 'So you threatened that if he ever mentioned it to anyone, you would make public that you and I knew he was involved in the whole mess.'

'I did. And he said in a small voice that I could be assured he never would. Then he told me something.'

'Is this the good bit?'

Rupert nodded. 'MI6 surveillance decided to keep an eye on Eric Mildew for a few days, to make sure he went quietly. Last night he was spotted boarding a flight to Tehran.'

'Hmm... I doubt that will do him much good. He's not been in a position to do the Taliban any favours for a few years now. He won't have many friends there.'

'Exactly.'

'So is all this properly over now?'

'I think we can finally breathe easily.'

Half an hour after Rupert left, Maisie and Brutus walked in through the kitchen door.

'Oh, you're back then?' she said curtly.

'Nice to see you too, Maisie. Coffee?'

'If I must.'

'Maisie?'

'I'm not very happy with you, dear.'

'Me?'

'Well, both of you.'

'What have I done?' said Aidan innocently.

'You both lied to us, for one thing.'

'Us?'

'Yes, Brutus and me. He hears everything you know, lies and all.'

'Oh yes I forgot. Of course he does.'

'And he's intelligent enough to know when people aren't telling the truth.'

'Um... he is?'

'Yes. And so am I, believe it or not.'

'Have we ever lied to you, Maisie?'

She snorted, to make a relevant point. 'Yes. Many times, actually.'

'Maisie!'

'Don't look like that. As I said, I knew full well you hadn't gone to Cornwall.'

Daisy glanced uneasily to Aidan, who narrowed his eyes. 'How could you know that for sure, Maisie?'

'I just do. And I'm quite certain I know where you did go.'

'Um... so where *did* we go, according to you?'

Maisie took a sip of her coffee, using the time as a pause for dramatic effect. 'You went to meet up with that Chinese girl.'

Daisy threw a seriously-concerned glance to Aidan. 'How... how can you be so sure?'

'I am quite well aware of Aidan's fetish. You went to see her and those naturalists.'

Daisy let out a sigh of relief, trying her best not to let it show. 'The word is naturists, Maisie.'

'Whatever. The point is you buggered off there and you didn't take me with you, despite me telling you I wanted to go the next time. I'm really pissed with you for that.'

'Um, Maisie... we didn't go to the Lake District.'

'Oh really... more lies then.'

'No, actually we went to the Caribbean in secret, on a military flight to Venezuela. Then on the way to Trinidad in a battered old fishing boat we hit a hurricane and the captain jumped ship, so we had to ram a beach before the fuel ran out. Then our friend was kidnapped by pirates, so we had to fight our way into the jungle to save her. Idiotic Aidan got captured too, so then the rest of us had to free them both, with the help of a tribe of monkeys who were being schooled by a robot teacher. Then the robot got killed, the pirates got caught... and here we are.'

For a moment Maisie stared at them without saying a word. Then she grabbed Brutus's lead and headed for the door.

'Maisie?'

She glanced back as she stomped onto the drive. 'I've never heard such a load of codswallop in my entire life. The lengths you two will go to, just to excuse yourselves for not inviting me. You don't deserve my company. Goodbye.'

'But...'

Aidan grabbed Daisy's arm. 'Let her go, Flower. She'll calm down later.'

'I can't do right for doing right.'

He chuckled. 'In truth, if she's the only problem we've got left, we're not doing so bad.'

Daisy picked up her mug. 'I'll go see her later, and make peace.'

'A bunch of flowers and a box of chocolates might help.'

They chinked mugs, and then Daisy threw Aidan a cheeky look. 'It might take more than that, dear. We might have to think about taking her on an actual *naturalist* event next time.'

Aidan shook his head. 'And there was me thinking it was all over.'

We hope you enjoyed 'The Pointing Finger'. We'll be eternally grateful if you can spare two minutes to leave a review. It really is very easy, and makes a huge difference; both as feedback to us, and to help potential readers know what you thought.

Thank you so much!

Catch the 2022 Christmas Special, 'Here Comes Santa Claus!'

Celia, Jack, Sarah and Rob are enjoying Christmas Eve supper at Fern Cottage with Daisy and Aidan. It's a lovely evening, until just before midnight when Santa drops in.

His appearance is a little unexpected, to say the least. Aidan is forced to eat his earlier words that "this time they'd made it as far as Christmas Eve without anything unusual happening"... but they don't realise just how much of a feast he'd made for himself until Christmas morning dawns.

A worrying discovery leads the Henderson Detective Agency to the conclusion their particular Santa maybe isn't so much into the holiday spirit!

As events unfold faster than Christmas itself, it becomes clearer still that Santa and his band of elves are anything but jolly...

'Here Comes Santa Claus' is released in all bookstores, and will also be available direct from our own website, in time for Christmas!

Why not give our new series a go?

The Sandie Shaw Mysteries is a 1920's murder mystery series set in Chicago, and is now lots of books old!

When Sandie witnesses her client committing a cut-and-dried murder, her head tells her to walk away. Her heart tells her she can't. It's a life-changing decision. Without knowing it, she's heading for murky waters, and there's no turning back...

Sandie is available in all bookstores now!

AND DO COME AND JOIN US!
We'd love you to become a VIP Reader.

Our intro library is the most generous in publishing!
Join our mail list and grab it all for free.
We really do appreciate every single one of you,
so there's always a freebie or two coming along,
news and updates, advance reads of new releases...

Go here to get started...
rtgreen.net

The RTG Brand

The RTG mission in life is simple... to not be like everyone else!

'Going Green' has taken on a new meaning, in the book world at least. Whilst we applaud the original meaning (ebooks are a perfect way to promote that) we also try to present a different angle to it.

The tendency these days is that if you don't look and read like everyone else, you don't sell books. Maybe there's *some* truth in that, but we simply don't do it. The RTG books have been described as a 'breath of fresh literary air', and, by those discovering us for the first time, 'unexpectedly good'. We know many readers prefer the same-old same old, and that's fine.

It's just not what you get from the RTG stable.

Those who know about such things said it would take five years to become a proficient author... I scoffed at that. They were wise. It took six. It's one reason why even today we remodel existing books, and will always do so. Right from the early years the stories were always good, but were put into words less well than they could have been!

These days we have several series and a few standalones, the hit Daisy series most popular amongst them. In everything we do, the same provisos apply –

1) Never the same book twice.
2) If we can't think up a good story, it doesn't get written.

The RTG brand is about exciting and twisty plots, a fast pace which doesn't waste words, and endearing (sometimes slightly crazy) characters. We can never please everyone, but it works for us, and, it seems, for those who appreciate our work.

Enjoy! Richard, Ann and the RTG crew

Printed in Great Britain
by Amazon